PRAISE

"Thor, Baldacci, Flynn, Hamburg. Get ready as Banner fits right in!"

AMAZON REVIEW

"Move over Jack Reacher there's a new guy taking over."

AMAZON REVIEW

"Great stuff. Exciting and fast paced. On par with Flynn & Thor."

AMAZON REVIEW

"The writing was superior, the story line was compelling and the action was top-notch. Sorry I could only give this one a five star rating!"

AMAZON REVIEW

INVISIBLE EVIL

A HARRY BAUER THRILLER

BLAKE BANNER

RIGHTHOUSE

ISBN-13: 978-1-63696-319-8

ISBN-10: 1-63696-319-6

Cover design by: Damonza

Printed in the United States of America

www.righthouse.com

www.instagram.com/righthousebooks

www.facebook.com/righthousebooks

twitter.com/righthousebooks

HARRY BAUER THRILLER SERIES

For neither man nor angel can discern
Hypocrisy, the only evil that walks
Invisible, except to God alone.

John Milton, *Paradise Lost*

ONE

THE MOON, EVER A LIAR, PRETENDED TO SMILE. TO ME it looked like the smile of a radiant corpse. She was suspended, apparently weightless, over dense trees and bushes at the end of the garden; a fall moon, the trickiest of them all.

It was an early September night. We sat at a round table on the lawn at the back of the Cobra HQ, near Pleasantville, where nothing is what it seems. The table was set with white linen, the candles stood in eighteenth-century silver candlesticks that once belonged to Napoleon Bonaparte, the knives and forks and spoons had allegedly been used by Thomas Jefferson while he was plotting to secede from the British Crown, and the eight flaming bamboo torches that squared the circle around us, keeping the bugs at bay, were from Amazon, at forty-two bucks ninety-nine per set.

The food and the wine were not from Amazon. Brigadier Alexander "Buddy" Byrd had a chef who'd been with him for twenty years or more and was to sauces and roasting what Mozart was to flutes and pianos. Nobody knew his name, nobody had ever seen him, but he was a legend to those who had dined with the brigadier.

The brigadier managed to sit at the head of the table, even

though the table was round. It was not so much a case of where he sat, but the way he sat there. I guess he carried so much gravitas he distorted space so that round became oval. He was in a black dinner suit that probably cost as much as my TVR Griffith. The bow tie alone was so exquisitely understated it was all you could look at.

Unless you happened to be looking at the colonel. The colonel was in a black, sleeveless, strapless number I kept hoping would obey the laws of gravity and drop to the lawn. But it just clung tight to her body and smirked at me. She had a thin string of diamonds around her throat that, especially by candlelight, was distracting because it made me want to gnaw on her throat the way trolls were supposed to gnaw on bones.

A man in a white dinner jacket emerged from the house followed by two very pretty girls in French maid uniforms. The maids delivered plates of avocado and smoked Norwegian salmon to us and the man in the dinner jacket, whose name was Aitor, poured the wine, a *Marques de Murrieta, Castillo de Ygay,* 1986, which I knew came in at around six hundred and thirty bucks a bottle, plus tax.

The brigadier was saying, "You need a full-bodied white with a strong, oily fish like salmon. The whites from Rioja are greatly underrated."

"*Because* they're full-bodied," added the colonel, and I stifled a yawn by reaching for my whisky. "And, call me a philistine," she went on, "but that allows you to have it that little bit colder."

"I agree."

"I don't," I said. "I think you're a philistine."

She stared at me a moment, in shock, but when I smiled she laughed. I turned to the brigadier, who was spearing a piece of salmon and trying to skewer a piece of avocado with it.

"If we were at a restaurant in New York," I said, "I might convince myself that you'd invited me here because no sparkling dinner would be complete without me. But the fact that we are doing this at Cobra HQ makes me suspect you have some other reason, like a job."

He looked at the colonel, eyebrows arched and smiling, like she'd said something surprising. She smiled at her food and scooped a piece of salmon and avocado without piercing either of them, which just goes to show that women are smarter than men.

"I wish," he said.

"What's that supposed to mean?"

"Jane and I were discussing a job just last week. We were saying it would be right up your street. Unfortunately it is completely outside Cobra's remit. There would be absolutely no justification for giving you that job."

I carefully folded a piece of salmon, pierced it and put it in my mouth, then picked up a piece of avocado with my fingers and popped that in too. When I'd chewed, swallowed and sipped my wine, I raised an eyebrow at him.

"So your intention was to get my interest. You have it. Now you are going to have to explain."

He dabbed his mouth. "Some might say that what we do is technically illegal. On the other hand, I would argue, if I had to, that we are instructed by the executives of the Five: the United States, United Kingdom, Canada, Australia and New Zealand, on matters of national security which are beyond the jurisdiction of the courts, and, technically, it is *not* illegal. So, we occupy an ambiguous, gray area on the fringes of legality, because it is in the interests of national security of the Five. And all of that is for a simple reason—we deal in assassination, as opposed to murder."

"Meaning it's politically motivated."

It was the colonel who answered. "Political in the sense that our targets affect, or are capable of affecting, the balance of world power. Politics," she gestured at the brigadier, "as Alex is always saying, is the practice of accruing and *retaining* power. We are tolerated and retained by the Five precisely because we help to maintain the balance of power. We are in effect a covert, political weapon."

She reached for her glass and the brigadier took over, as though they were a couple of well-rehearsed TV presenters.

"But if we once started taking out targets because we had a vendetta, because they were standing in the way of the political ambitions of one of our clients, or indeed because we personally disapproved of them in some way, then we would be on the very slippery slope toward perdition."

"Who is this person, and what have they done?"

The colonel had her glass halfway to her mouth. She paused and set it down again.

"You have to understand, Harry, that we *cannot* ask you to do this job. And if you were to decide to do it, we could not pay you or bail you out if you got in trouble. You could not contact the brigadier or me for the duration of the job. As far as we are concerned, you would be on holiday somewhere."

"You make it sound so attractive. What's the downside?"

The brigadier took a deep breath and sat back in his chair.

"I am not a religious man, Harry. I try to take a philosophical, empirical view of the world. But this man..." He stopped, frowning at one of the torches that flickered in the September breeze, casting moving firelight across his face. "This man is evil. There is no other word for it. One can try to understand him from a psychologist's point of view, one can argue that good and evil are human constructs that do not exist in nature..." He shook his head. "I don't care. Whatever the circumstances that created and conditioned this man, he is now the incarnation of evil. He is evil made human, flesh and blood."

"What's his name?"

The colonel said, "I doubt you've ever heard of him. He is not famous. He is an American citizen, and killing him would be murder, plain and simple."

"What's his name?"

"His name is Oscar Larsen, known as Oz. In his youth he was a member of the Hell's Angels, but," she started to laugh, and by candlelight that was a nice thing to watch, "they asked him to leave because he was out of control!"

The brigadier laughed quietly and continued. "For the last few years, nobody is really sure how long, he has had his own gang. The basic requirement for joining seems to be that you are either a psychopath or a sociopath, and that you find ordinary organized crime too restrictive."

"Gang," I said, "what kind of numbers are we talking about?"

The brigadier looked at the colonel, who was mopping her plate with a slice of bread. She finished, sipped her wine and sighed. "It is very hard to be precise. He has ten to twelve men who seem to go with him everywhere. By which I mean, he might go to the bar down the road with all of them, or two of them, or four or six of them, but the others will be at home or within a couple of minutes if he calls them. But in addition to those twelve, he has a number of," she looked at the brigadier, "what would you call them?"

"Followers, disciples? It's very much like a cult. There are maybe twenty of them, fifty, a hundred? We don't know."

"Do they have a name?"

The colonel replied. "Apparently they call themselves simply Free Men. They have acquired a few nicknames in the local underworld, Ozwalds, Ozones..."

"How come I've never heard of these guys?"

"Because they keep a very low profile, and they are on the other side of the continent."

"California?"

"Not quite, southern New Mexico."

"Halfway across."

"It was a manner of speaking, Harry. The reason you have not come across them is because they keep to themselves, the press tends to steer clear of them, much like everybody else, and they are located halfway across the continent."

Aitor appeared again with his two pretty maids. They took away our empty plates, and the empty bottle of wine, and returned shortly afterwards with a large steak and kidney pie, a bowl of roast potatoes, Vichy carrots and buttered broccoli. To accompany this feast there were two bottles of red *Marques de Murrieta, Castillo de Ygay* 2001, which came in at a very modest two hundred and fifty bucks a bottle, excluding tax. It was like drinking ripe plums and whipped, full fat cream, with the added benefit of alcohol. It seemed a shame to spoil it talking about Oz, so we ate in silence till our plates were almost empty, and our stomachs were in a stupor of distended pleasure.

Then I sat back and sipped and sighed and said, "So, what has Oz done that has singled him out as the only human on Earth Cobra would stoop to murder for?"

The brigadier arched an eyebrow at his last remaining potato. "Nicely put. I'll tell you."

He put the potato in his mouth, set his knife and fork at six o'clock, the way Brits do, wiped his mouth with his napkin and concluded operations by sipping his wine.

"Oscar Larsen was born in Nogales, in Arizona, in November of 1981, which makes him forty years old. His mother was a prostitute and, without the benefit of DNA testing and a great deal of patience, his father's identity must remain a mystery. He, Oscar, was in and out of foster homes throughout his childhood and, at sixteen, he left home and became a prospect for the Hell's Angels."

He swirled his wine for a moment, sniffed it and then sipped it. After quietly smacking his lips he went on.

"As you probably know, when you are a prospect for the Hell's Angels you are required to do absolutely whatever you are told to do, even if that means taking the fall for a member and going to prison." He paused and smiled. "Oz did not take the fall for anyone. He was told by one of the senior members of his chapter that he, the senior member, was going to kill a member of the *Chupacabras*, a Mexican motorcycle gang not dissimilar to the Angels, and that Oz was going to have to take the fall and go to prison. This would involve serving a sentence of at least sixteen years."

The colonel took over while Aitor and the pretty maids cleared the table and delivered a cheeseboard, a bottle of twenty-year-old Courvoisier and another of the Macallan.

"Of course, if that senior member was caught and tried he could face the death penalty. But a boy of sixteen, his first offense, a good defense lawyer paid for by the Angels and good behavior, Oscar's sentence could be as little as sixteen years, of which he would probably serve thirteen.

"However, what Oz did was to tell the senior member to go to hell. If he was going down for a murder, he said, he would go down for a murder he had committed, not for one somebody else had committed. So he went to a bar where he knew the *Chupacabras* hung out, found the intended victim, stuck him with a ten-inch blade and disemboweled him right there in the middle of the bar.

"In court he pleaded guilty, contrary to his attorney's advice, but said that he had heard on the grapevine that this man planned to kill *him*, and he decided on a preemptive strike."

The brigadier poured me a glass of whisky and as I cut myself a slice of Stilton he continued the story.

"Oz served thirteen of the sixteen years. His first two years he got into several fights with the most feared and dangerous gang leaders in the prison. I assume he did that deliberately. He knew he had the backing of the Angels, but apparently he didn't care either way. What he wanted was to make sure everybody inside feared him, even the screws. And by the time he was eighteen he was universally feared. Nothing went down without his say-so, and he took a percentage of everything that came into the prison, booze, tobacco, drugs.

"By his third year he had settled down to an apparent life of good behavior. But this was in reality because anything he needed done, he got one of his boys to do it for him. So after eleven years of living like a king and running the biggest organized crime ring in the history of the prison, he was released early for good behavior."

The colonel balanced a piece of brie on a cracker and slipped it in her mouth, then picked up her glass.

"Two weeks after he was released, the Angel he was supposed to take the fall for was found dead, disemboweled in his house. He had been castrated and had his eyes gouged out. The Angels never managed to prove it was Oz who had done it, but they revoked his membership and made him leave.

"He soon surrounded himself, however, with the worst and most psychotic members of the Tucson underworld and, within a year, he had taken over the drug importation racket north of the border. He agreed terms with the Sinaloa cartel and secured exclusive distribution rights for anything coming into Arizona from Mexico."

The brigadier was nodding. "But that was not enough for Oz. For him, you see, it was not really about the money or the expensive cars or any of that. For him it was all about sticking it to the authorities. More even that that, I would say it was a challenge to himself to see just how evil he could be, just how far he could push the limits of his own inhumanity before anybody tried to stop him.

"He never challenged Sinaloa, because they were a source of enormous wealth and power for him. As the Angels had in their day, Sinaloa gave him a very valuable backing. But what he did do was to go far beyond simple drugs trafficking. Pretty soon he had moved into the prostitution and pornography industry, and within five years, using the money he was making from distributing for Sinaloa, he had moved into white slaves, not just from Mexico, but from Poland, Russia, the Philippines and Brazil. He owned a string of discreet, luxurious gentlemen's clubs in San Diego, Yuma, Phoenix and Tucson and that was where he exploited these girls.

"He was good, and he had disposed of at least half a dozen

rivals. He was thorough and meticulous, and nobody was ever able to pin anything on him."

I was steadily working my way through the Stilton and the whisky, enjoying the little act they had prepared for me, but asking myself what was so special about this guy. In the end I interrupted.

"This guy, I agree, he's a son of a bitch and the world would be a better place without him. But there are thousands of guys like him. We can't just take it upon ourselves to start eliminating them all, one by one, much as I would like to."

The colonel shook her head. "That's what we said to you in the beginning. But what we are telling you here is just a little background so you understand how he got started. By the time he was thirty-seven, in 2018 or thereabouts, he had established himself as the most dangerous gangster in Arizona and Southern California, and nobody, outside the FBI and the local PDs, had ever heard of him."

The brigadier nodded, then looked at me. "But what he did next was what eventually put him on our radar."

TWO

THE TEMPERATURE HAD DROPPED AND THERE WAS A slight, agreeable chill in the air. The colonel had wrapped a light stole around her shoulders and was holding her glass of cognac in both hands, watching the brigadier, apparently content to let him take over the story for now. He helped himself to a little more cheese.

"As I said, Oz was making enormous amounts of money, but the thing for him was never the cash. What motivated him, what excited him, was breaking the rules, pushing the boundaries and going as far beyond what was acceptable to any normal human being as he possibly could. So what he did was to set up a website, offering child pornography. He employed a couple of geeks to run the site and, I am no expert in these matters, but apparently, by using several VPNs, they were able to make it almost impossible to locate the server from which the site was hosted. In other words, for anyone trying to track them, they might have been in China, Russia, Mexico or in the middle of the Pacific Ocean in international waters. At this point all Oz did was to buy videos from stock that was available on the web.

"But in 2019, he made a major move. He relocated his HQ up into the mountains above Eden, and, as well as that, he set up a studio in the desert. The studio was separate from the HQ. It was essentially a prefabricated hangar kitted out as a basic film studio, and they would go there every couple of months or so, and make films. He had studied his market and knew what his punters were prepared to pay top dollar for. From there it was a short step to creating his own channel."

I had stopped eating and was studying my whisky. I muttered, "Now I'm beginning to understand." I frowned, "Wasn't there some Arab guy arrested and prosecuted for something similar recently?"

He shook his head. "I'm not sure. But I don't think you fully understand yet, Harry. Most child pornography relies on rings of parents who have brought their children up in that environment. That is sick and odious enough, but what Oz did next went well beyond that."

I could feel the burn growing in my belly.

"Where is this guy now?"

The colonel glanced at me and murmured, "Wait, Harry, you need to hear all of this."

"He created teams," said the brigadier, "whose task it was to travel the country—here and in Mexico—identifying vulnerable children, and in some cases families, and kidnapping them or luring them here for the purpose of exploiting them. I need hardly say that what they looked for was children who had never been exposed to this kind of nightmare. What he sought to capture with the camera was the fear. Fear and submission is what this monster is hungry for."

I set down my glass and snarled. "I thought the Feds were supposed to be on top of this kind of thing. Isn't this what they're there for? How the hell can they allow something like that to happen?"

He nodded. "I'm afraid, Harry, that sometimes the law is a self-defeating institution, because it has to protect people's rights and freedoms, and obey its own rules. The operation went on for over a year. The Bureau knew it was going on and they were monitoring it, but they were unable to get the kind of evidence they would need for probable cause. They had a team trying to identify where the HQ and the studio were located in the hope of being able to raid them. But they had very little success, until a field agent in Arizona informed them that he believed Oz was running some kind of operation in the hills north of Eden. Efforts were intensified, but they were still unable to identify a studio, or gather anything remotely like probable cause to raid the HQ."

"So what happened?"

"A team of federal agents eventually managed to follow four of his gang to the studio in New Mexico. They now had a location, but still nothing they could take to a judge and ask for a warrant. So, in frustration, they took matters into their own hands and broke into the studio after the gang members had returned to HQ in Arizona. They took photographs and video footage of everything they could find and grabbed computers, laptops, films—everything you could hope for. Their plan was to deliver it anonymously to their own team. That way the person acquiring the evidence would have committed a felony in breaking in and stealing it, but the investigative team would be off the hook and free to adduce it as evidence to the court."

"Good, what happened?"

"They committed that most cardinal of sins. They underestimated their enemy. He had concealed motion-activated CCTV cameras all over the studio. He filmed and recorded every move they made and every word they said." He paused, then intoned, "'If you know your enemy and you know yourself, you need not fear the result of a hundred battles. If you know yourself but not the enemy, for every victory gained you will also suffer a defeat. If you know neither your enemy nor yourself, you will succumb in every battle.'" He shrugged. "Obviously they had not read their Sun Tzu, and every bit of evidence they acquired was ruled inadmissible by the judge, and the case was kicked out of court, defeated before it had even started."

"Who was the judge?"

"Judge Casper Williams, but he only did what any judge in America would have been obliged to do, apply the law to the facts. It is, if you will forgive me saying so, one of the more asinine features of an otherwise sound legal system. By all means, punish the agents—punish them severely if you will—but the evidence should be judged admissible or not on the basis of its probative value, not on how it was acquired. Still, there it is. On the evening of the hearing in chambers, Oz was out on the streets of Tucson celebrating at the Three Points Casino."

He fell silent and after a moment the colonel said, "Of course, on the upside his operation had to stop, but on the downside he is now free to start another one. And knowing him, it will be even worse than the previous one."

I stared at her. "How could it possibly be worse?"

The brigadier grunted. "You've been in Helmand, use your imagination."

I went cold inside. I felt my skin crawl, and I knew that as long as that man was alive he would not stop pushing the limits of his own evil.

"What do the Feds say?"

He took a deep breath. "The Federal Bureau of Investigation says that the law must be upheld and enforced at all costs and under all circumstances. An alleged, un-attributable source claims that the team who were investigating Oz's operation are certain that his success has emboldened him and he is preparing a new operation in New Mexico. He has moved there, to Manuel Vazquez County, which is about as remote and isolated as you can get in the United States without moving to Alaska, and he has bought a property about thirteen or fourteen miles northeast of Dell City, about seven miles north of the Texas state line, as the crow flies, and not very far from his old studio. Rumor has it that he still has stuff hidden there."

I said, "If he's gone that remote it's because he doesn't want to be seen."

"Obviously."

"And if the Feds or the Sheriff's Department go anywhere near them, his lawyers will slap them with every kind of injunction known to man, and probably sue for damages into the bargain."

The colonel nodded. "You can bet your bottom dollar on it."

"And within the month this bastard will be preying on children again, not only with impunity, but protected by the law."

The brigadier refilled our glasses. "In a nutshell," he said, "yes."

"So, if I accepted this job which you are not offering me, how would this work?"

The colonel leaned forward and placed her glass on the table.

"For a start you would have to understand that you were committing murder, and there would be no get out of jail free card for you here."

"I get that."

"Second, whatever files you may remove from the brigadier's office, or mine, during your visit, cannot be traced to us and do not have our fingerprints on them."

"I understand all of that," I said, "what I need to know, in real, practical terms, is to what extent can you help me? Logistically, how much useful information can you give me—names, addresses, numbers, locations—and how do I get to this bastard?"

"In real, practical terms, I have a file with all the relevant information on where he is and what he is doing, to the best of the Bureau's understanding—which is not a great deal, and that is on my desk because I have forgotten to put it away. As to how do you get to the bastard..." He made a question with his face which involved raising his eyebrows and looking at the colonel. "Jane?"

"Wait," she said, "let's take one step at a time. In terms of weapons we cannot provide you with any hardware."

The words were incongruous coming from such a feminine face, decorated with diamonds and bathed in candlelight. I tried not to smile. If she noticed she ignored me.

"Whatever weapons you need you will have to secure either from your private arsenal or from a private supplier. In Arizona and New Mexico that is not going to be a problem. Now—" She looked at her glass and turned it around a few times, like she was looking for the best angle. "As to how you get to him, physically, he has a property about three and a half miles northwest of Hope, which is a census designated place about twelve miles northeast of Dell City. It's a farming community. There are about three hundred and fifty inhabitants all told. You can stay at the saloon. It's called the Horns of the Dilemma. There's not a lot else to tell about the town."

The brigadier said, "Oz lives at his property. It's called the Farm. Apparently they get whatever they need from the town. Sometimes they pay, sometimes they don't."

"What about the sheriff?"

"Sheriff Matías Olvera, he's based in Vazquez, the county seat, about fifty miles northwest of Hope by winding road. They get a lot of stray sheep up there, so he has his hands pretty full. From what I hear, the last time he went to Hope was about two weeks after Oz moved in to the Farm, about six months ago. He hasn't been back since."

"Right." I nodded. "He's not going to be a problem, then."

"I wouldn't have thought so."

The colonel drained her glass and slid it across the table toward the brigadier. As he refilled it she said, "Now, your main problems are two: first, how many men are you up against? We have zero reliable intel on that. It is unlikely to be less than twelve, and unlikely to be more than a hundred."

I laughed. "You're kidding."

"Not really." She shook her head. "Crazy cults like these can end up attracting a lot of people. What's the membership of the Hell's Angels? Two or three thousand? Koresh had almost a hundred people on his ranch when the Feds stormed it, and Bhagwan Shri Rajneesh had two thousand people living at his so-called Rancho Rajneesh, in Oregon. We just have no idea what he has going on out there, but whatever it is, it has the allure of plenty of money, sex, drugs and rock and roll."

"OK, understood, and my second problem?"

"Your second is going to be getting enough reliable intelligence to develop an executable plan. They are reclusive, largely self-reliant, well organized and they have the people of Hope terrorized. So getting reliable information will be difficult and dangerous." She raised a finger and nodded as another thought came to her. "*And*, he is IT literate and has skilled nerds working for him. He may be operating in Hicksville, but his techs are up to the minute."

I grunted. Neither problem was insurmountable. "What we're talking about is a period of recon and then developing a workable plan. That's standard operating procedure."

The brigadier nodded. "Yes, but in the kind of environment we are looking at here, in a standard operation you would have the support of three other blades. In this case you are alone. And I do mean alone. Much as we would like to, we *cannot* help you."

"You don't need to keep telling me that, sir, I understood it the first time. You drummed it into me in the Regiment. Never get into a fight you don't know you can win. I'll recon. If it's doable, I'll do it. If it's not, I'll nuke the place."

He smiled, put his hands on the arms of the chair and stood.

"I'd expect no less from you. I must excuse myself. And, Harry, my study is unlocked and I have a very sensitive file on my desk, with a duplicate beside it. Be a good chap and don't go in and filch it, will you?"

"I wouldn't dream of it, sir."

"Good night."

We watched him go inside, then sat in a silence that could have been comfortable and companionable, or uncomfortable and awkward, depending on how much you had drunk. I hadn't drunk enough. I gave her the kind of smile you give someone when you're not sure whether to smile or not. It didn't matter much because she was staring at her glass and didn't see it.

"Are we done talking about not-work?"

"Yup." She gave a single slow nod at her glass.

"Can I ask how you've been? I half expected you to quit.[1] You haven't been in touch."

"No," she said, with unnecessary ambiguity. I waited for her to clear up the ambiguity but she just kept staring at her glass. Eventually I asked her, "No, I can't ask how you've been, or no, you haven't been in touch?"

"Alex, the brigadier, whatever, he told me what you did." She looked at me and frowned. "What you went through. I am very conflicted, Harry. I feel guilty."

"What about?"

She gave a quiet laugh and offered me a sardonic smile.

"Come on, Mr. Tough Guy. I know you play the indestructible man of iron, and I know to some extent it is real, but I also know you're human, and I know you suffered a lot. Not just physically. I know you went through a lot of anxiety too..."

Before she could finish I nodded and interrupted. "Yeah, that has a name, Jane." She paused and eyed me. I said, "It's called life. If you live in a three-dimensional, physical world, there is going to be pain. It's as unavoidable as time and space. We don't get to choose on that score. What we do get to choose is how we deal with that pain." I shook my head. "You won't hear me talk like this very often, so you had better pay attention, Colonel. If somebody I care about is in trouble, then I choose to deal with that pain by fighting to help that somebody. And I'll do whatever I have to do."

"Harry..."

"Wait. I'm not done. Your family were threatened and you did what you had to do to protect them. You should not feel guilty about that. You did the right thing. The only place you screwed up was in not telling me from the start."

She frowned and returned her attention to her cognac. "Thank you." She said it like she wasn't really sure. "Harry, you said," she hesitated, "you said 'a person you cared about.'"

---

1. See *Breath of Hell*

"Yes."

"Do you mean care about as a friend?"

I sighed. "Honestly, I don't know."

"That can't be."

"I know. But we can only control how we behave, Jane, not how we feel."

She took a deep breath, seemed about to say something, then smiled an empty smile and said, "I had better go up."

She stood and I stood with her. She placed a hand softly on my chest.

"Good night, Harry. And thank you, for everything."

If she hadn't kissed me softly on the cheek, I don't know what I would have done. But she did, and that killed anything else that might have happened. Then she brushed past me and disappeared inside. For a moment I almost went after her, but the impulse never became action. Instead I sighed very deeply, sat back down under the sneering moon, and poured myself another dram of solace.

THREE

I took my Jeep, an overhauled 1999 Cherokee, and drove via Ohio, Indiana, Missouri and Oklahoma, then cut through the Panhandle on the I-40 toward Albuquerque. At Santa Rosa I turned south on Route 54, and felt for the first time I was in New Mexico, with the long, straight road plunging south through a yellow desert of dry grass and shrubs, under a menacing sky.

I passed White Sands and Alamogordo, and a bunch of road-side diners, motels and gas stations with flying saucers parked nearby, and after almost three hours I came to the intersection with the Owen Prather Highway and turned east. That part of New Mexico along Route 54 already feels a little isolated, despite the tourism attracted by the UFO stories, but when you turn east, toward Vazquez County, things get real remote. The vast, open spaces, the miles of scorching, parched desert, the emptiness, all become paradoxically claustrophobic. It feels like the burning emptiness is closing in on you, and there is nowhere to escape.

I followed the highway through barren flatlands for fifty miles, and then started climbing into the southern foothills of the Sacramento Mountains as the sun declined behind me, turning them an eerie shade of lavender pink.

I bypassed the tiny town of Vazquez at just before eight. It looked like a grid of dusty roads peppered with dilapidated wooden houses and pickup trucks. I put thoughts of homemade burgers and ice-cold beers out of my mind and kept going. I crossed the hills and connected with State Road 506, south, and after that it was an hour through growing darkness in absolute wilderness, under a translucent sky with more stars than you could dream of, peppering infinity with tiny shards of ice.

When I finally reached Hope it was after ten at night and all the lights in town were out, with a few notable exceptions. There were four ancient streetlamps posted along Main Street, that looked more like extremely tall, one-eyed aliens than lighting appliances. They cast a lugubrious, orange glow that didn't so much illuminate as create shadows, in which cars slept behind black windshields.

I passed scattered houses, each sitting in its own dustbowl. Here and there a razor of light sliced through closed drapes. The church on the corner of Vazquez Avenue lay dormant under the weight of its own cross. Then there was the auto repair shop, which looked like a mechanical massacre littered with steel bodies. But next door there was the Abandoned Hope Saloon Bar. As I cruised past I read the inscription under the sign. It said, "Here Shall Ye Find No Salvation but Liquor." The lights were on and the music was drowned out by the voices and the laughter inside.

Next, on the corner of White Sands Road, was the Horns of the Dilemma Inn. The entrance was at the top of seven steps at the corner of the building, forming a kind of triangular porch with a longhorn skull fixed over the doors.

I parked out front, grabbed my shoulder bag from the back seat and my kit bag from the trunk and climbed the seven steps. The doors under the horns were blond wood and glass, and gave on to a dimly lit lobby with a desk and an office on the right, a lounge with TV on the left and stairs directly ahead. Two potted plants segregated the lounge from the lobby. The TV was on, but nobody was watching it. I whacked the bell with my open palm.

Something moved in the office and a man in his seventies came out holding a newspaper. He peered at me over his reading glasses and whatever he saw made him frown. He said, "Yes?"

"Henry Brennan, I booked a room."

His frown deepened. "Oh, yes. People don't often book rooms here. Can't think why anyone would want to come here at all, 'less they had to."

He approached the desk, grabbed a ledger from below and put it in front of me. There was no computer. "Sign here," he said, pointing. "Room three oh-four. Third floor, end of the passage on the right." He took a key from a pigeonhole behind him and dropped it on the ledger. "How long will you be staying?"

I took the key. "I'm not sure. Maybe a week or so."

He stared at me a moment. "Mostly we get traveling salesmen, and a few seasonal laborers who work on the farms down in Dell City. We have a couple of men in the town who ain't married, and we do for 'em." He paused. I didn't say anything so he came out and asked. "Mind me askin' what brings you to this particular corner of hell, Mr. Brennan?"

I smiled. "I don't mind you asking, Mr...?"

"Jones. Me and my wife own this place, my parents and grandparents did before us."

On an impulse he held out his hand and I shook it. "Bill," he said, "William Jones atcher service."

"How do you do," I replied. "I'm a writer, Mr. Jones, and I have a contract to write a novel which is set down here in the southwest. But my wife, whom I adore, never stops talking, so I packed up my laptop, climbed in the old Cherokee, and drove here from New York to find some peace and tranquility, so I could work."

He hunched his shoulders and a big smile transformed his face. He wheezed a laugh and leaned back toward the office.

"Hey, Hanna!" he said, laughing, "Mr. Brennan here just

checked in, says he drove all the way from New York to get away from his wife's talkin'!"

He threw back his head, opened his mouth wide and for a second remained like that, in silence, before releasing a huge cackle. As he leaned forward and slapped his thigh, a woman who was maybe ten years younger than him appeared at the door. She had the dark eyes and complexion of a Mexican and was still handsome in her sixties. She regarded him with long-suffering amusement, then shook her head at me.

"You couldn't send your wife to Miami instead?"

"So she could spend the advance before I've even written the book?"

She came forward and took the ledger. "You're writing a book?"

"Trying to."

She nodded, but her big eyes said she didn't believe me.

"I don't know how much peace and tranquility you gonna find around here, Mr. Brennan. You might have been better going up to Maine, like Jessica Fletcher. People round here think we are still in the Wild West. They never got the memo, you know?"

"Well, I'll give it a try for a few days and see how it goes. Any place I can get a meal around here at this hour?"

She made a doubtful face. "You got the saloon across the road. They make burgers and steaks. The food is good, but the company is not so good, especially on Friday and Saturday night. A lot of noise, sometimes there are fights." She pointed to the lounge. "We got a small dining room through there. Breakfast between eight and nine, lunch between twelve and two, dinner from seven till nine." She shrugged. "Now the kitchen is all closed up."

"That's OK. I'll get something at the saloon. Thanks."

"Back before twelve, please, Mr. Brennan."

I carried my bags up to the bedroom, slung the kit bag under the bed and made my way down again. Mr. and Mrs. Jones had transferred to the lounge to watch a movie and I stepped out into the New Mexico night. There was a cold breeze that made me shudder as I crossed the road, but the saloon, as I pushed through the old wood and glass door, was warm and noisy. The air was heavy with smoke and the bar and most of the tables were occupied. I was surprised for a moment there were that many revelers in the town. Then I realized that most of them were wearing leathers. Those who were not bald had long hair, and just about all of them had some kind of beard. This was a biker gang.

There were women, too, mostly young, mostly drunk. A few people turned and watched me walk to the bar, but on the whole they ignored me. The bartender was big, in his thirties, but he didn't have the look of a biker. His eyebrows twitched at me, registering that he didn't know me.

"What'll it be?"

"Beer. Is it too late for a burger?"

"The works?"

"Sure."

He walked to the end of the bar, opened a door and yelled in, "Burger, the works! Yeah fries, of course fries!"

Then he came back and poured me a beer from the tap. As he handed it over he gave me a meaningful look. "You want the table in the corner?" He glanced over my shoulder at a corner of the room where there were less people. He shrugged. "It can get a bit noisy."

"Sure. Appreciate it."

I sat in the corner and sipped my beer, and while I did that I counted the guys in the bar. There were ten of them, though they were making enough noise for three times that number. Most of the talk seemed to be related to either sex, drugs and alcohol, feats of exceptional violence or bikes. I wondered where the bikes were, and figured there must be a parking lot in back.

I had studied the file I'd taken from the brigadier's office, and I'd had a good look at what photographs there were of Oz. I scanned the faces in the saloon and was satisfied he wasn't there. Which meant he was somewhere else. And if he was somewhere else that meant he had to have a dozen more of his goons on hand. So he was either somewhere else in Hope, and these were his praetorian guard, or he had another twelve men as well as these.

The burger arrived and I ate it staring at my phone like I was reading something. Meanwhile I focused on the noise and tried to filter out the irrelevant and see if I could pick up anything of interest. I didn't—until I'd put the last piece of burger in my mouth and was preparing to drain my beer. Then I heard the word "Jones."

I put down my beer and picked up my phone again, and tried to zero in on the conversation. The voice was bordering on the hysterical, laughing and shouting.

"They are crazy, man! How can anybody still, like, *be* like that? He's so, like, 'I'm a wise old country man, with glasses!'"

I looked for the voice and found him standing beside a table, doing a stupid old man walk with an idiot expression on his face. There were three guys and two girls at the table who were helpless with laughter.

The clown started talking again. "But the wife, man, she is *old*, like sixty or something, but I could so take her, man. I bet she was hot when she was a *señorita*."

There were shrieks from the girls and cries of "Man, you're sick!" from the men. He ignored them.

"But the real cutie is the daughter. Have any of you guys seen little Maggie?"

Someone shouted, "Oh, yeah! Man, she is hot!"

"I want Maggie for me!" The clown bellowed a Tarzan-like cry and beat his chest. "I'm tellin' you. I am going to go over there and tell them, 'Mr. and Mrs. Jones, I want your daughter's hand... *on my dick!*'"

This elicited hysterical laughter from everyone. I wondered how serious he was, or whether he was just mouthing off. In my experience that kind of asshole mouths off until he builds up enough of an obsession to do something about it. As I made my way to the bar to pay he was repeating:

"I am going to do it, man! I swear, I am going to *do* it!"

I paid and walked through the chill night back to the hotel. When I stepped through the door I found them sitting in the lounge watching TV. They nodded and smiled, then turned back to the TV. I hesitated, then stepped between the two potted palms.

"Mr. and Mrs. Jones, do you have a daughter called Maggie?"

They exchanged glances. He answered, "Why would you ask a thing like that, Mr. Brennan?"

I sat, facing them. "Because the bar I have just come from was full of," I paused and took a deep breath, "what appeared to be members of a motorcycle gang." I watched them exchange glances again. "They were very drunk, most of them, and they were making a lot of noise. But just before I left I heard one of them, he seemed to be the clown of the group, make a comment about 'Jones.'"

I saw Hanna's hand go to her mouth, and her husband went a sickly gray color. He said, "What has that got to do with Maggie?"

"Because this same clown said that the Joneses had a daughter called Maggie. I have to tell you that the way they spoke about you and her worried me. It made me worry for your safety."

Unconsciously they took each other's hands. He appealed to me with his eyes.

"What can we do? I'm almost eighty. Hanna is in her sixties. Maggie don't live here. She's over the border, in Texas."

"You should tell her to stay away until this gang leaves."

Hanna leaned forward. "We have told her, but they are not going to move. They have settled here. They live at a ranch north of Hope. We told Maggie, 'Don't come here any more!' but she says, 'I am not going to go and visit my mommy and daddy?' She is headstrong. So she comes and she visits, and I am so scared for her."

"Have you talked to the sheriff?"

Mr. Jones scoffed. "That no good piece of chicken shit? First day they showed up he shit his pants and hightailed it up to Vazquez. We ain't seen hide nor hair of him since."

I nodded, trying to think. I was about to say something about contacting the state authorities in Alamogordo when there was a sudden noise out on the street, like a mob or a riot, but it was peppered with shrieks and laughter, and then drowned out by the roaring of a large number of big motorbike engines.

I looked Hanna in the eye. "Hanna, I need you to do something. I need you and your husband to run up to my room." I handed her the key. "My shoulder bag is on the bed. If you open it, at the bottom you will find a semiautomatic pistol. I need you to bring that down for me. I will meet you on the stairs. Then I need you and your husband to go upstairs and lock yourselves in my room. Understood?"

They stared at me in horror for a moment. I said quietly, "We haven't got a lot of time. If I am going to face those boys, I'd rather do it with a 9mm in my hand."

Hanna stood and snapped at her husband, "Come on, Bill, hurry!"

They hurried up the stairs and I stood listening to the noise outside. There was a lot of shouting, and a lot of revving of a lot of bikes. Then suddenly a bunch of them, maybe half or more, took off into the night, leaving the rumble of maybe three or four bikes outside, along with the murmur of voices and occasional laughter. After a moment a voice behind me said, "Hey, Mr. Brennan!"

I turned. It was Hanna, gingerly holding my Sig Sauer P226. I took it and as she hurried back up the stairs, I cocked it and slipped it into my waistband behind my back. Outside I heard some whoops and shouts, then the unmistakable voice of the clown screaming, "*Hey Momma Jones, little Bobby's comin' to play with you!*"

I stepped out onto the porch and leaned against the wall at the top of the steps, looking down. There were four of them. They had their bikes parked across the street and they were walking toward the hotel. The clown was at the front, on his right side he had a guy with a red headband, long dark hair and a big moustache. On his left was a guy with a big gut and a big mess of blond hair and beard all over his head, and bringing up the rear was a bald buy with a goatee. They saw me and slowed as they approached the steps.

I said, "Mrs. Jones is not available. You boys best go home and sleep it off."

The clown said, "Who the fuck are you?"

And the bald guy behind him said, "He's the guy who was eating a burger in the bar before. He was watchin' you. I saw him."

I walked slowly down the steps till I was looking down into the clown's face, less than three feet away. His maw was slightly open.

"Maybe you didn't hear me, Bobby. I said, go away."

He leered, still with his mouth open, and I saw his hand go for the knife hanging from his belt.

Punching from a neutral, standing position is not as hard as many people think. I bent my right knee, projected my right hip forward and drove a straight right pile into the side of his chin. I felt the joints of his jaw snap and his inarticulate scream tore the cold night in half. As he fell back into his pals I pulled the Sig from my belt and put a round through the hairy blond's temple and waved the gun at the other two as the big slob sagged to the dust.

"Back up. Hands in the air." They backed up, eyes and mouths forming six perfect circles. When we were on level ground with no corpses between us, I said, "You were going to rape a woman tonight."

The bandana jabbered, "No, no, we was just foolin' around..."

The instep of my boot smashed into his groin, crushing his testicles. While he doubled up, whining, I shot the bald guy through the middle of his forehead. Then I shot the red bandana in the temple. As I turned to go back toward the hotel I saw Bill standing at the top of the steps with a double-barreled shotgun, staring at me. We stood like that for a moment till he said, "Sweet Jesus," and after a moment, "Who in the hell are you?"

I stepped up to the clown and stamped on the back of his neck with my heel. He stopped whining.

"I told you. I'm a writer."

FOUR

I PULLED THE JEEP ROUND, OPENED UP THE BACK AND dropped the seats. Then I heaved the dead meat in. It wasn't easy, but Bill was stronger than he looked and he gave me a hand. At one point he cackled and said, "Least there's no fear of the sheriff showin' up! Ha!"

And as we shoved the last one in he said, "Where you gonna take 'em?"

"You tell me."

He shrugged and made a face. "Well, there's the Guadalupe River, comes out of the Guadalupe Mountains to the east of here, runs southwest till it meets the Rio Grande at the Mexican border. There's a track." He pointed east down Main Street. "It goes all around the White Sands Flats and meets up with Williams Road outside Dell, 'ventually." He gave his head a little twitch. "River's pretty deep there, where it comes down out the mountains, 'specially this time of year, and where it crosses those flats, it can get pretty marshy. I reckon a body's either gonna get swept all the way down to the Gulf of Mexico, or it's gonna get buried in mud an' silt."

"Sounds good to me."

I slammed the back of the Jeep and yanked open the driver's

door. Bill scowled at me. "You're gonna need help. You might get lost out there, an' that fat bastard must'a weighed three hundred pounds if he weighed an ounce!"

I hesitated. I knew he was right, but my instinct told me I shouldn't leave Hanna alone. He must have read my mind because he shook his head.

"They'll be back, mister, for sure, but not tonight. I'll lock up tight, and we'll be back before dawn."

I nodded. "OK, thanks."

He hurried inside and emerged a couple of minutes later. He locked the doors and hurried down the steps to join me in the Jeep.

We followed Main Street to the end, where it intersected with the Vazquez Road, but there, instead of turning north, we turned south onto a broad track of beaten earth. In the fanned light of the headlamps the road looked a ghostly, luminous white. And either side of the road, what I could see of the landscape was flat and almost featureless, dotted with gnarled shrubs. On my left the massive hulk of the Guadalupe Mountains rose ink-black against the translucent sky. On my right there was an eerie, translucent white glow. I jerked my head at it.

"What is that?"

"Salt flats and white sand. Th'say the Gulf of Mexico came right up here, through Corpus Christie and Del Rio, way back, an' left deposits here. I don't know about that, but it's as soulless a desert as I ever seen. Flat an' white and dry. They say it'll dry a man out inside an hour. Kill him inside three."

We drove on for about fifteen minutes, taking it easy, and eventually Bill leaned forward in his seat, squinting. I slowed and he pointed up ahead. "Bridge is just here on the right. You can see the river yonder, comin' out the mountains."

He was right. The river, a broad band of luminous foam and reflected starlight, could be seen cascading out of the steep hills on the left, three or four hundred yards away. It plunged into a deep gull and passed beneath the road. The bridge itself was raw concrete with three-foot walls either side. I pulled in on the right and killed the engine and the lights.

The doors echoed like gunshots in the dead of night, above the quiet roar and hiss of the river as it churned beneath us. I yanked open the back and dragged the first of the bodies out. It was the guy with the red headband. With Bill's help I hoisted him onto my shoulder, planted my right foot on the parapet, leaned forward and let gravity do the rest.

He vanished into the darkness and, after a moment, we heard the muffled splash as he was sucked into the maelstrom below. We nodded at each other and went for the next body.

The next was the clown, and then the bald guy. It was hard work. These guys were strong and weighed on average two hundred and twenty pounds each. But when it came to the big slob with the wild hair and beard, we couldn't shift him. So I backed up to the parapet, climbed in and pushed the bastard out with my feet. He hit the concrete wall with an ugly thud, then rolled and plunged into the churning, foaming waters below.

When I climbed out Bill pointed at my shoulder. "You got blood on you, son."

I looked and saw big, dark smears all over my shirt. I pointed back at him and smiled. "That's a job for you and Hanna tomorrow. My shirt, and the back of the truck, bleach, more bleach, and then some more bleach."

"You got it. That ain't no problem. Hell, I don't know how to thank you enough."

We climbed in and slammed the doors. I turned the truck around and headed back to Hope.

"Don't thank me yet," I told Bill as we got underway. "There will be reprisals." I glanced at him and saw he was staring at me with narrowed, searching eyes. "You and Hanna may have to go visit Maggie for a few days. Can you do that?"

"You ain't no writer," he said.

I gave a single bark of laughter at the road ahead. "No?" I

asked. "What the hell am I doing in this godforsaken neck of the woods then?"

He didn't answer, but he smiled all the way back to Hope.

My instinct, when we got there, was to leave the large bloodstains in the dust on the road outside the hotel, as a message to Oz and his boys that from now on there would be a price to pay for their excesses. But for once my gut had to yield to my brain. Because I knew I would not have to face the backlash on my own. Bill and Hanna would have to face it with me, and I could not let that happen. So before we went up to bed, in the translucent, lying light of the moon, we scraped up the bloody mud and put it in refuse sacks, then swept the dust and the gravel over what was left. I figured a forensic team might find the remaining blood, but nobody else would.

I got to bed at gone three and slept till eight, then rose, had a cold shower and a shave and made my way down to the small dining room, where there was a table laid for me. Hanna bustled out of the kitchen when she heard me arrive and sit down. She didn't meet my eye but rattled as she straightened my napkin, my knife and my cup, "The farmers are all gone, they have their breakfast early, but now I can make you a good American breakfast, eggs, bacon, sausages, waffles, or a continental if you prefer, we weren't sure if you were going to be up early, seeing as..."

She trailed off. I smiled. "American with all the trimmings would be good, with lots of black coffee. How's Bill this morning?"

She shrugged, spread her hands, raised her eyebrows, all in rapid succession.

"Fine!" She said it like it was an outrage and he had no business being fine. "Great! Singin' and whistling this morning like an eighteen-year-old kid. I washed your shirt."

"Thanks."

"Lots of bleach."

She stared at me with a rigid neck for a second, like she was strangling whatever it was she was trying to say, or not to say.

Then she blurted out, "I'll go get your breakfast. You must be hungry!"

She hurried away, back to the kitchen, and I sat for a while wondering if I should, or could, have done things differently that night. My mind offered no answers. It was a blank, except that however many men Oz may have had yesterday, today he had four less. That made me smile.

A while later Hanna came out with a plate big enough for Dumbo, piled high with four eggs, half a pound of bacon, four sausages, mushrooms and two huge slices of whole-wheat toast.

"I thought probably you were hungry."

Bill came in behind her with a large pot of coffee and two cups.

"We're gonna join you, Mr. Brennan—"

"Harry—"

"Harry, then, because Hanna wants you to answer some questions."

She made a tight line of her mouth, clenched her fists and gave a little stamp. "Oh, Bill, I told you, 'No—'"

"Come on, woman." He sat, filled my cup and poured a cup each for him and his wife. "Sit down and let's have this out. If it were not for this young," he paused and stared at me under his eyebrows, "writer, we would probably not be alive right now, and you would have gone to heaven minus your virtue. But tell him, tell him what's on your mind." He paused and frowned at me a moment, with his cup halfway to his mouth. "Sorry, Harry, probably spoilin' your breakfast."

I shook my head and cut into the first of the four eggs. Hanna sat with her hands clenched in front of her apron, and watched me eat, as though it was the saddest thing she had ever seen.

"We got two daughters," she said.

"Two?" I managed, with my mouth full. "Where's the other one?"

"San Diego. She's a doctor. She works at the Jacobs Medical Center. She's only twenty-eight but she was gifted at school."

Bill pulled a wallet from the pocket of his cardigan and took out a photograph which he slid across the table for me. I laid down my knife and fork and picked it up. It showed a pretty blonde, slim, with bright, alive eyes. She was dressed in a white coat and had a stethoscope hung around her neck. She had an indefinable air of class about her.

"She's pretty," I said and handed the photograph back. "She must be smart, too."

"Very smart," said her mother.

Bill was already handing me a second picture. I took it. The girl in this one had wild red hair cut to shoulder length. She had freckles and very blue eyes that wanted to play. She was grinning, dressed in dungarees and was holding a hay bale beside a flatbed.

"That's the other one, Maggie. I inherited a ranch from my dad. It's not a big ranch, only small, but she runs that and makes it work."

"You're very lucky," I said. "You have two wonderful daughters."

"They are both wonderful," said Hanna. She held me with her eyes while I cut into the sausages, pleading with me not to make her say it. I sat back and chewed.

"It's normal that you are afraid for them, Mrs. Jones—"

"Hanna, please."

"But you have to understand something about these men. They have no inhibitions. They have no limits. There is nothing in their minds telling them where they have to stop. The man who came last night with his friends, Bobby, he had already made up his mind about what he was going to do. Forgive me if I am blunt, Hanna, but it is important that you understand. Your life might depend on it. He had decided to rape you, and if your husband had tried to protect you, they would have had no hesitation in killing him. But you have to realize that he had also already made up his mind to rape Maggie."

I paused to stick some egg, bacon and toast in my mouth and sat chewing, watching her, with the coffee halfway to my mouth. I swallowed and sipped while she tried to assimilate what I had told her.

"What I did last night changes things only a little. What will happen now? Now Bobby will not rape you or Maggie."

She looked up at me and frowned, like she hadn't thought of that. Bill chuckled. I went on.

"But his gang will come looking for him and his three friends."

She clenched her hands so tight that her knuckles went white. "And what are you going to do, Mr. Brennan, Harry? Are you going to leave us? How can we protect ourselves?"

I looked at her for a long moment while I chewed slowly on the bacon. Then I took in Bill's worried face.

"Are you sure you want to know the truth?"

They exchanged a glance and she said, "Yes. We have to know the truth."

I gave a small nod. "Then understand this, Hanna. I am not going to leave this town until every single one of them is dead."

They were completely silent as they watched me eat, like they were having trouble with the way reality had suddenly changed for them. Finally, as I mopped the last of the egg from my plate, Bill said, "Some writer."

I leaned back and sipped my coffee. "I don't like bullies."

He leaned forward, pointing at me. "Look, Harry, I watched you last night. I was standing on the steps. You didn't know I was there. And you was just like, bam-bam, two down. Then it was, 'Back up,' bam-bam, two down. It was—" He shook his head, looking around the room for the right word. "*Efficient*," he said at last. "It was efficient. Like watching a pro doing his job."

"I was in the army."

"Yeah, right. So was I."

"Look, Bill, it's best you just accept that this is the way it is. Nothing happened last night. I came back from the bar, I went to my room, you watched TV. The bikers left. We got up in the morning and had breakfast. Don't dig, don't ask questions.

Nothing is going to happen to you or your daughters. Maybe—" I hesitated a moment and Hanna refilled my cup. "Maybe at some point in the next day or two it would be a good idea if you and Maggie went to visit your other daughter—"

"Heather—"

"Heather, in San Diego."

Hanna nodded a couple of times and looked at her husband. He shrugged and looked disappointed. She turned back to me and said, "We can do that."

"Good." I stood. "I'm going to go for a drive."

They both watched me but remained seated. Bill said, with just a hint of sullenness, "Goin' to seek some inspiration, huh?"

"Yup. May I suggest you call both daughters this morning, and talk to them?"

Bill sighed and they both stood as Hanna started to clear the table.

I made my way out to the street and was about to climb into the Jeep when I saw the barman from the night before, standing in the door of the saloon, watching me. I crossed the road, raised a hand and saluted him.

"Morning."

"Morning."

"I was wondering," I said, "did you hear any commotion last night, after your patrons had gone?"

He pulled down the corners of his mouth and shook his head.

"I'm much like the other folk in this town, mister. I have bad eyesight and poor hearing, and my memory don't work so good neither. Must be somethin' in the white dust round here."

I watched his face a moment, trying to read what it was telling me. I smiled on one side of my face, where it didn't really look like a smile.

"Rumor has it four of those bikers were killed." I turned and pointed at the intersection. "Right there, not twelve feet from the hotel."

His face was about as informative as a utility bill. "Is that right?" he said.

"But you know what's weird?"

"Nope."

"They say it was just one man who killed all four of them."

He looked away. "You don't say?"

"They say it took him all of ten seconds, and not a trace of the bodies. What do you think of that?"

"I don't think nothin', mister. And I don't care for gossip."

I nodded. "You're a wise man," I told him. "A fool might go running off at the mouth, and get himself interrogated by those biker boys, and then killed by whoever butchered those animals last night."

He didn't say anything. He just stared into my face.

I said, "Do we have an understanding? I'd like to feel sure that we have an understanding."

He nodded. "Yeah, sure we have."

"Good. That's good to know."

I made my way back to the truck.

FIVE

It was about five miles from Hope to the Farm, where Oz and his boys had made their HQ, through some of the harshest terrain I had seen anywhere outside of Afghanistan and North Africa. The earth was flat, composed of fine, pale gray dust, almost like talcum powder, sparsely dotted with gnarled sagebrush and yucca, as far as the eye could see. And the sky at the horizon was not blue, but scorched white.

The Farm, when I finally caught sight of it, was in reality a compound. It lay about one hundred yards east of State Road 506, roughly five hundred yards square, with two electrified chain-link fences running parallel around the perimeter. I didn't approach the place. I pulled off the road about half a mile away. I had found a long depression where the shrubs were a bit denser, as though it might form the channel for a stream during the floods in the fall. I pulled the Jeep into a hollow, where it was more or less out of sight, climbed out of the truck and took my rucksack with me.

I lay on my belly in the hollow among the shrubs and pulled my binoculars from the bag. That was when I saw the double fence. I figured there were about six or seven feet between one fence and the other, and I could see Rottweilers loose in there. They weren't patrolling with handlers, they were just lying around, eating and sleeping in the morning heat. That wasn't as stupid or as careless as it seemed. If those fences were electrified, even if you managed to get through the first one, those dogs would be on you within seconds, and you'd have no way out— and no handlers to pull them off.

I scanned the tops of the fences. There were cameras at every corner and at the halfway posts. Inside the compound, beyond the perimeter, there was a lot of empty, flat, dusty space, and roughly at the center was a large house flanked on either side by what must have once been stables and barns, but were now, presumably, garages for the bikes—and, I guessed, a film studio. Unless, as before, they had set up the studio elsewhere.

They also had, to the right of the buildings, a large dish antenna. Maybe it was so they could all watch TV, but somehow I didn't think so.

I enumerated in my mind the immediate problems I had. The first would be approaching the compound unseen, and the second and third were two sides of the same coin: getting inside and getting a clear idea of just how many men there were inside the compound. What was the size of the enemy force?

It was clear the approach had to be at night. Though, having said that, I told myself, I was pretty sure the compound would be floodlit from dusk till dawn. Still, after dark I would at least be able to get closer than half a mile.

Even if I could get close enough at night without being seen, getting inside was going to be a whole different ball game. For a start, any breach of the outer perimeter fence was going to trigger an immediate response from the dogs, and anything up to a hundred raving psychopaths on motorbikes would descend on me in seconds.

So if I couldn't go through the fence, I would have to go either under or over. A tunnel would take too long and simply wasn't practical. Which left over. And that begged the question, how the hell do you elevate yourself over a twelve-foot electrified fence in the middle of the flattest desert on Earth?

And, at the same time, manage to remain unseen?

On the one hand, it was pretty clear we had Manuel Vazquez County pretty much to ourselves as our homicidal playground, but it was also pretty clear that if we started lobbing bombs and missiles at each other over their perimeter fence, the state authorities would probably notice and send in the National Guard. I thought of the colonel, and smiled.

It would have to be something subtle, something ninja.

On the other hand, the dilemma was something of a vicious circle, because mode of entry depended on what kind of response I was going to get once I was inside. And I couldn't know what response I was going to get *until* I was inside.

I sighed as I scanned the compound. There was another incognito: how many innocents were in there? Did they have women, kids? If I could be sure there were none, that would open up all kinds of possibilities with explosives.

But I could not be sure of anything like that. Right then I was like damned Socrates. I only knew I knew jack shit.

I pulled a digital camera with a telephoto lens from my bag and took a closer look at the buildings themselves, taking pictures as I went. There was a large house at the center of the complex. It was on three floors and I figured right then I was looking at the back of the house. There seemed to be building work going on, and I could make out about a dozen men wheeling barrows, laboring and mixing cement. There was also a medium-sized excavator that appeared to be digging a large hole.

To the right of this there was a horseshoe-shaped building with a gable roof. The open end of the "U" was toward me and that was what I figured had once been stable and was now a garage-cum-workshop-cum-storehouse.

I took some more pictures and scanned to the left. There,

there was just open ground, an old derelict barn and a couple of troughs for animals. There were no people that I could see, no activity except the building work, whatever that was.

I panned back to the garage, pausing along the way to count the laborers at the back of the house again. This time I made it ten. But when I focused on the garage I saw six more guys in leathers mounting their bikes, and a bald guy standing talking to them. I took a string of ten photographs, then slung my stuff in the back of the truck in a hurry and headed back toward Hope.

There was a good chance the six bikers were on their way to look for the clown and his pals, to see what had happened to them and why they hadn't returned. I sure as hell didn't want to be lying in the shrubs with a pair of binoculars in my hands when they drove by. As it was they didn't overtake me, and when I got back to the hotel there was no sign of the bikes. There was just a beaten up twenty-year-old red Toyota pickup out front. I parked beside it and swung down from the cab, wondering if I was too late for lunch.

As I rounded the hood and made for the hotel steps I saw a man approaching from the saloon. He was about six foot in his cowboy boots, had a Stetson hat on his head and a belly that said he had lived not wisely but too well. He also had a star on his Wrangler shirt. He raised a hand.

"Mr. Brennan?"

"Sheriff."

He gave me an ingratiating smile. "I was hoping I'd run into you. I'd like to have a word if I may."

I didn't return the smile. "What about?"

"You're new in town."

"I'm not new in town. I'm here for a few days, hoping to get some material for a novel I'm writing."

"Uh-huh, a novel. Good." He smiled a fat smile. "I look forward to reading it. So, uh, I understand you was at the saloon last night."

"Briefly. I'd been traveling long hours and I hadn't eaten. The hotel dining room was closed, so I stepped into the saloon for a burger and a beer." As he drew breath I interrupted him. "Sheriff, I don't mean to be uncivil, but how is this of any interest to the sheriff's department?"

"Well, I'm comin' to that, Mr. Brennan. I understand when you was in the bar, there were some members of a motorcycle club in there too."

"Yes, they were making a lot of noise, so I finished my food and left."

"Did any of them come after you?"

I frowned and smiled at the same time. "Come after me? If they had I'm pretty sure I wouldn't be standing here talking to you right now, at least not without a few bruises."

He laughed. "They did not approach you or talk to you?"

"No."

"And did they enter the hotel, after you had, I mean?"

I shook my head. "Not to the best of my knowledge, no." Then I added with some emphasis, "Why?"

"Well, four of those boys have gone missing. Last time they were seen they said they planned to come to the hotel to, um, talk to the owners."

I narrowed my eyes at him. "Sheriff, isn't it a little early for that? These are four young men who are members of a pretty wild motorcycle club. It has barely been twelve hours since the events you are talking about, and they looked to me as though they were very capable of looking after themselves. They are probably sleeping it off in some brothel near El Paso."

He narrowed his eyes back at me. "You did see them, then?"

"Of course I saw them, Sheriff. I just told you I had a burger and beer in there, and I left because they were so noisy. And I'll tell you something else, if the man you are talking about, who said he wanted to talk to Mr. and Mrs. Jones, is the one I think he is, he did not say he planned to talk to them. What he said was that he planned to rape Mrs. Jones, and her daughter."

The sheriff turned pink and started laughing again. "Oh, well, young drunken fellers say all kinds of crazy things. Don't mean we need to take 'em seriously!"

I took a step closer to him and frowned down into his face.

"Let me see if I understand you, Sheriff. Four young men in their late twenties and early thirties, members of a motorcycle gang, absent themselves for twelve hours and you feel it's your duty to investigate. But one of those gang members declares his intention to rape two women, and you dismiss that as unimportant. Do I understand you correctly?"

"No! No, nono, no, that was not what I intended to...no. We, I, the sheriff's office just received an inquiry from...," he waved his hand in a circular motion, "friends of the, err, missing boys, and I thought I'd just drop by and ask around."

I studied his face a moment. "Did you know, Sheriff, that the people of this town are afraid of the members of this gang?"

"You been here just over twelve hours and you already know that, Mr. Brennan?"

"Yes. But don't let me hold you up, Sheriff Matías Olvera, you have some," I paused and loaded the words with heavy irony, "missing persons to find. They did not come to the hotel last night, and they did not attempt to rape Mrs. Jones."

He nodded and looked uncomfortable. "No," he said. "Sure, well, you take care, Mr. Brennan, and don't go gettin' involved in things that ain't your concern. That's what the sheriff is here for. Understood?"

I watched him back up a couple of steps, waving his hand in a weird mix of farewell and admonition. I shook my head.

"No. I'm a writer, Sheriff Olvera, we have to get involved, in all sorts of things. Be seeing you."

I turned and climbed the steps up to the door, still hoping I wasn't too late for lunch. As I pushed through the door I was greeted by raised female voices. Bill was standing behind the reception desk with his elbows on the counter and his chin in his hands. From the office I heard a young woman saying, "I *can't,*

Mom! Do you know how much work I have on the farm? I can't just walk away and say, 'Hey, yeah, I know, I have a full harvest to take care of so I'll go to San Diego for a few days to visit my sister who never writes or calls!'"

Hanna's voice rose above her daughter's. "Don't talk like that about your sister! You know she works so hard as a doctor!"

"Doctor, doctor. Jesus! Like I don't work hard as a damned farmer!"

She stormed out of the office and stopped dead, staring at me. She wasn't wearing dungarees. She was wearing jeans and a red-and-black-checked huntin' shootin' fishin' shirt. Her hair was tied back and her face was flushed pink. She radiated health and irrepressible vitality the way the sun radiates photons.

I said, "Hello."

"Hello. Dad?"

Bill didn't look around. He sulked into his hands and said, "What?"

"You have a customer." She pointed at me and I realized she was holding a straw cowboy hat. "He is standing right there, staring at me."

I smiled. "You must be Maggie."

"I guess I must."

"I'm Harry."

"Oh."

I stepped forward and extended my hand. "I am renting a room here. Your parents and I have already made friends. They were telling me over breakfast how proud they are of you, managing that farm the way you do."

She hesitated a moment. Then smiled uncertainly, took my hand and shook it.

"They were? Shame they don't tell me sometimes."

Hanna had emerged through the office door and was looking at me. I glanced at her. "Am I too late for lunch?"

Bill said, "Inspiration made you hungry, huh?"

"You're not kidding. Why don't you join me? You can tell me all about your planned visit to San Diego."

The suggestion caused obvious embarrassment and awkwardness, but I made like I hadn't noticed, turned and walked toward the dining room. I heard Bill mutter behind me, "I'll set the places."

He and his wife disappeared into the kitchen. I sat and Maggie stood in the middle of the floor, looking from the kitchen to me and back again. Eventually she shook her head.

"I can't..."

I shrugged with my eyebrows and pulled the corners of my mouth down.

"I had a sergeant once who told me those were two words I should never use."

"Three."

"Cannot is one word, Maggie. You want to bring us a couple of cold beers?"

She sighed nasally and didn't quite flounce on her way to the kitchen. She re-emerged with two cold bottles and placed one in front of me. She looked like she might remain standing, but then pulled out the chair opposite me, sat and took a swig.

I did my best Kiwi accent. "You say you can't, Herry, whin what you mean is, you don't know how."

She regarded me with the expressionless face she'd inherited from her father. "Is that supposed to be inspiring? Am I going to tell my grandchildren about this moment that changed my life?"

"Probably not, but you and your parents are in serious danger and you need to get them out of Hope for a few days."

"What, now?"

"There's a gang, about five miles north of here, bikers."

"I know, the Free Men."

I nodded. "Mm-hmm. Last night, across the road in the saloon, I heard them talking. There was one of them, Bobby, who said he was going to rape your mother, and then you."

"Those boys are always mouthing off. They're full of shit. They never..."

"You're wrong."

Her face said those were words she had never quite got used to, even as a kid. Her cheeks flushed and she put the bottle back on the table. "Listen, pal, I don't know what your game is, but you arrived last night and suddenly..."

"I'm not a writer."

SIX

SHE STOPPED. THE NEGATIVE STATEMENT BEGGED THE question: If I was not a writer, what was I, then? And that was what she was asking herself right then.

I went on.

"I want to get this part of the conversation over with before your parents come out. After I left last night, Bobby and three of his pals came to the hotel, looking for your mother. They were drunk and they were stoned, and they were very dangerous."

"Jesus!"

"I have not come here to write a book. The leader of this gang, a guy who goes by the name of Oz, was prosecuted recently for various crimes including drug trafficking and murder. He got off on a technicality, because the evidence was illegally obtained. He is a very, *very* dangerous man."

"What happened last night?"

"Let's just say I persuaded them not to come back."

She gave her head a small shake that was all about incredulity and not negation.

"Have you got ID, some way of proving this shit?"

"No. But check your parents for bruises. They haven't got any."

The kitchen door swung open and Bill appeared with a tray of plates, glasses and cutlery. As he started setting them out on the table I looked him straight in the eye and grinned.

"Bill, tell Maggie what happened last night." He stopped dead and stared at me. I chuckled. "Skip the bit where I killed the four bad guys and we got rid of the bodies in the desert. But tell the rest of it how it happened, from where I got in."

There were three surprisingly long seconds where he just held my eye. Then he blinked and dropped the knives and forks on the table.

"Well, Harry here arrived late. The kitchen was closed. So your mom tells him he can go and have a burger across the way. I guess he was gone 'bout an hour. When he come in, we was watchin' TV in the lounge, and he says, 'I heard them motorcycle gang boys talkin' about your wife and your daughter.' He says to your mom, 'They're sayin' they want to rape you,' and he tells us we'd be smart to go up—" He stopped and glanced at me. "Should I tell her about the bag?"

"Sure."

"So he says, 'Bring me down a semiautomatic I have in my bag, then the two of you lock yourselves in my room.'"

Her cheeks flushed and her eyes went wide and round with anger. Bill plowed on.

"Well, we took him down his weapon, but I weren't gonna let him defend my wife alone. So I took my shotgun and I went down the stairs fast as I could. Left your mother locked in our room. And when I got out the door I sees Bobby and three of his pals standin' at the bottom of the stairs and Harry here leanin' cool as a cucumber on the wall, lookin' down at them. They're lettin' their mouths run an' he says, 'Mrs. Jones ain't available. You boys best go on home.'"

His eyes creased up and he started to wheeze with pleasure.

"Well, you should'a seen them boys' faces! Here's this dude, all alone, cool as hell, 'You boys best go on home.'" He laughed and Maggie looked mad, but she didn't say anything. "So then Bobby says, 'Who the eff are you?' So Harry here, real slow, like Dirty Harry, walks down the steps till he's standin' right over Bobby, and he says, 'Maybe you didn't hear me, boy. I said, go away.' Just like that. Next thing, Bobby reaches for his knife and Harry, quick as a viper, smacks him in the jaw, and before that boy'd hit the ground Harry had his semiautomatic in his hand and..."

He stopped dead. Maggie turned and glared at me. Before she could start her lecture I said, "It wasn't really that dramatic. I let them know that your parents had backup and support, and I sent them home, where they'd come from."

"Do you realize how dangerous it is to provoke these people?"

I nodded. "Yes, Maggie, probably better than most. But now I have a question for you. Do you realize what would have happened to your parents if I hadn't been here?"

Her eyes dropped and some of the anger drained from her face. "I suppose I should thank you."

For good measure, I added, "Your parents are not at risk because I defended them. They are at risk because that gang is dangerous, and nobody is keeping them in check."

She sighed and took a pull on her beer. As she set it down again she said, "So now what? We are at war with a dangerous biker gang, and when Dirty Harry goes back to wherever it is you came from, what do we do then? My parents have to confront this gang alone? What do we do?"

I gave her a moment, then said, "I don't know, Maggie. Why don't you tell me?" She mouthed like a shocked goldfish for a moment. "I do know one thing," I said, "I am not about to offer you or your mother up as a sacrificial lamb. Because, maybe I'm reading you all wrong, but it sounds like that is what you're suggesting."

"Of course I'm not!"

"So tell me, what should I have done last night? Should I have gone to my room and put earplugs in to shut out the screams?"

She looked away. "Stop it. You know that's not what I'm saying."

"So what are you saying?" I gave her a moment. She didn't say anything.

The kitchen door opened and Hanna emerged with a big bowl of rice, chicken and beans.

"You're going to forgive me, but I had this made already in the fridge, and all I done is heat it up. Maggie, *trae mas cerveza, cariño,* like we say in Spanish, I have a thirst of a thousand daemons!"

She sat and started dishing out food while Maggie did as she was told and went to get more beer. When she came back and sat down, I raised my bottle to Bill and then Hanna. "Here's to two exceptional people, Bill and Hanna!"

We drank and started eating. After a couple of forkfuls I sat back and started talking.

"A few years back, before I became a writer, I was in a special operations unit."

"I knew it!" Bill looked at his wife. "Didn't I say that? I *knew* it."

Hanna put her hand on his arm. "Let the man speak, Bill."

"We did a lot of work in Iraq and in Afghanistan. And, believe it or not, the situation in Helmand Province, in the south of Afghanistan, reminds me a lot of the situation here right now."

Maggie sat back and raised an eyebrow at me. "Helmand Province in Afghanistan reminds you of southern New Mexico."

It wasn't a question, it was just ironic. So I ignored it.

"It's a desert, very sparsely populated, where the only law is the law of the Taliban. What were the Taliban? Basically a bunch of thugs who cruised the desert terrorizing people, raping, murdering and stealing on the basis that they had more and bigger guns than anybody else.

"You may not believe it, but what happened here last night, I have seen happen a hundred times in tiny villages all over the Middle East, but especially in Helmand Province. Women, children and men watching in fear as a gang of thugs shows up and says, 'We want you.' It might be to a twelve-year-old boy who is now old enough to kill the infidel in the name of Mohamed, it might be a girl or a woman who has caught the eye of one of those bastards. The point is, they want, and because they are in a position to mete out violence, and nobody can stop them, the villagers have to shut up and watch while they murder and rape their way through the village."

Maggie was looking really unhappy.

"This is a pretty heavy conversation, Mr. Brennan."

"It's a pretty heavy situation, and we don't have a lot of time. The point I need you to understand is that with people like these, who believe themselves invincible and indestructible, if you don't stop them, they will not stop."

She flopped back in her chair and made exasperated gestures with her hands. "How? How can I...? How can we...?"

"You can't. But I can." I let that sink in for a moment, then added, "But I need you, all three of you, out of the way."

She sighed. "Hence San Diego."

"Hence San Diego. I cannot stress to you enough, Maggie, how badly at risk you and your mother will be in just a couple of days."

"Why?" She was still looking exasperated. "What has changed?"

It was my turn to sigh. "The FBI tried to prosecute Oscar Larsen, the leader of this gang, a while back when they were based in Arizona. The case fell through because of a technicality. Let's say that last night I convinced Bobby and his pals that the smartest thing they could do was to get the hell out of Dodge. Now Oz and his boys will be looking for Bobby and his friends. When they don't find them they will draw their own conclusions. Now, what was the last thing Bobby did before he disappeared? What was the last thing he *tried* to do before he disappeared?"

There was a very heavy silence at the table. Nobody said the words.

"They'll be back," I said. "They'll be back with a vengeance. And I don't want any one of you here when they come."

Maggie threw her hands in the air. "Jesus Christ! I have a farm to run! It's not like writing a goddamned novel! I can't just up and go and take the damned farm with me! I could lose my crops! That has financial consequences, *Harry!*"

She said my name with heavy irony, like it was my name's fault all this was happening. Maybe if I'd been called Alvin none of this would ever have happened.

I nodded like I understood and took a pull on my beer. As I set the bottle down I asked her, "Does Oz, or do his boys, know where your ranch is?"

She shrugged. "How should I know?"

"I met the sheriff just before I came in. He was looking for Bobby and his pals. I told him it was a bit soon for a missing person's investigation, given they'd been gone for only about twelve hours. He said that Oz had asked him to look for them. So, given that the sheriff is that anxious to help Oz, how long do you think it would take him and his gang to find out where your farm is, Maggie?"

She muttered into her lap, "I don't know."

"Well, I'm going to hazard a guess at about two minutes. And after they've paid you a visit, and asked you where your mom and dad are, what do you think the financial consequences will be for your farm?"

"OK, you made your point. But we can't go to Heather's in San Diego. We have to go someplace else."

Her mother stared at her. "Why?"

Maggie took a deep breath and closed her eyes. "Because, like you said, Heather is way too busy with her work at the hospital and we don't want to be worrying her. Also, if the sheriff can locate my farm, he can locate Heather's apartment and her job. We have to go some other place."

I shrugged. "OK, it makes no difference to me. Take a long weekend in Corpus Christie. Just get the hell out of Hope, soon, and don't let anybody know where you're going. Not even me. Leave me a number where I can reach you when it's all over." I paused. "And, wherever you go, don't make it obvious. Go to Vegas, Miami, Los Angeles, have a holiday."

We finished our lunch in near silence, then I went up to my room to have a shower, change my clothes and study the file, and the photographs I had taken.

I showered hot, then stood under the cold water for five minutes. I dried myself off, pulled on my jeans and lay on the bed, reading again the account of the FBI's original investigation; and as I read it I understood more clearly what the brigadier had explained. It had not fully registered before because I was not familiar with the area, but now, as I looked at the map, I saw it clearly. Though Oz had been based in Arizona, his studio was not. His studio had been in New Mexico, in Manuel Vazquez County, on the border with Texas. Looking at the map, it was about ten miles west of where we had dumped the bodies, and ten miles east of Dell City. About three hundred miles as the crow flies—or the light aircraft—from his place above Eden.

He was obviously familiar with this area, with its extreme remoteness, and that was what had brought him back here. Like the brigadier had said, aside from Alaska, it was about the most remote place in the United States. It was typical of the man that, having been busted here, he didn't run to Mexico or Canada—or Alaska—he moved back to the very place where he'd been busted, and set up his new studio just a few miles from the original one. That said something about his character. It said that defiance was the name of the game: disobedience, defiance, and extreme evil.

But it also got me thinking. There was another, more pragmatic reason why he didn't want to stray too far from the original studio. It was probably the same reason why he had kept the studio and his headquarters apart in the first place. The brigadier had said there was a suspicion he had stuff hidden at the studio, and if that stuff was found by the authorities he had a better chance of washing his hands of it if it was not at his home. He could claim ignorance, blame the guys who worked there, distance himself from it.

And that made me wonder, if there was something to this suspicion and he had been hiding stuff at the studio, was it still there? Was he lying low, waiting for things to cool off before he recovered it, in case the Feds were watching the place? Maybe it was wishful thinking, but then again, maybe it wasn't.

I read the report again. The agents had busted into the studio. Working in haste and in the dark, they had managed to gather enough incriminating evidence to put Oz away. But hampered because they did not have a warrant, they had not done anything like a detailed search.

And that was a more compelling reason for why Oz was still here. Because he still had stuff at the studio that he wanted to recover. What? Cash? A stash of films? A stash of coke and heroin? Documents that proved his connection with the site? There was one simple way to find out.

I swung my legs off the bed, put the file away and pulled on my jeans and my boots, and my shirt. I put my gun under my arm and my Fairbairn and Sykes fighting knife in my boot. I was going to visit the movie studios.

SEVEN

It was like something out of a movie by Sergio Leone. Hundreds of square miles of creamy, white clay, battered by an incessant wind, covered in small, gnarled bushes of sage-brush, with exhausted green leaves and pale yellow flowers. The road, chalk-white, endlessly long and straight, cut through the afternoon heat haze toward the massive wall of the Guadalupe Mountains. The only movement out there was the listless, desultory wind, and the occasional shrouds of dust that it dragged up like ghosts from the grave, and trailed across the plain.

On my left, between two tall telegraph poles, a track led south through low dunes and shallow hollows, to a dilapidated cluster of shacks and prefabs behind a dry, peeling wooden fence.

I nosed into the track and followed it, pulling a huge white cloud behind me. I rolled in through an open gate and entered a rough, makeshift yard set between a low one-storey house, a huge wooden barn and a row of sheds. Behind the house, maybe twenty yards back, there was also a large, pre-fabricated metal hangar. It was bright red and had a vast, blue rolling door.

I tucked the Cherokee behind the sheds, where it was invisible from the road, swung down from the cab and closed the door. The Jeep, which had started out military green, was now the color of pale gray clay. There was a high-pitched moaning coming from the wires down by the road, and somewhere on the house a shutter had come loose and was squeaking on rusty hinges. Occasionally it would bang, too, as it was slammed closed and then fell open again.

I crossed the yard, with the wind tugging at my clothes, and tried the door. It was locked. I tried the shutters over the windows at the front, but they had been fastened from the inside. I paused and listened to the incessant, iron squeak. It was coming from the rear of the house.

I walked the length of the building, shielding my eyes from the dusty wind, and turned the corner. A cloud of fine dust reared up against the large hangar. The blue door rattled in the breeze. It was a listless sound, like the rusty squeak that now sounded louder and closer. Beside the hangar there was a silo, and a hundred yards from that an ancient water tower. In front of the tower there was another long shed, and this one had the door open. It moved back, then forth in the blustery afternoon. Then the wind caught it and banged it closed. It swung back open again, showing just how pointless it all was. But it didn't squeak.

What was squeaking was the open shutter halfway down the back of the house, as it moved back and forth in the irregular gusts of the wind. I walked to it, took a hold and examined the latch. The dry wood had been gauged away and the latch had been forced. The gauge was not worn smooth, or eroded with friction; the wood was fresh, blond, not gray and weathered. It was recent.

Inside, the window which the shutter had been put there to protect was also open. One of the glass panes had been shattered and the latch on the inside had been released. All the broken glass, I noted, was on the inside. I peered in. It was a bedroom, maybe twelve by twelve. There were two steel beds. Neither had a mattress. I pushed the window open, hopped onto the windowsill and dropped into the room.

The silence was oppressive. The gusts of wind that buffeted the house, and the shutter with its incessant squeaking, were somehow locked outside and failed to disturb the stillness within. I hunkered down among the broken glass. There was a thick layer of dust on the floor, but it was hard to tell whether there were footprints or not. There were scuff marks, but they didn't tell me any more than I had already learned from the busted latch and window. I stepped to the door and opened it. It was some kind of living room.

A threadbare, beige carpet covered the floor. The walls were the color of bile, with water stains, presumably from where the rain had leaked in during the thunderstorms that regularly hit the area from September onwards. There was a dark green vinyl sofa, cracked, with bits of yellow foam rubber showing through. A red easy chair and a brown vinyl armchair flanked the sofa around a wood and glass coffee table and magazine rack that had been fashionable when Neil Armstrong first walked on the moon. There was a window across the room. It had a Persian blind over it, and on the other side of the glass there was a wooden shutter. So only hazy light filtered in.

More light came from the kitchen, which I could just make out through an arch over on the right. On the left, a door stood open onto a second, darkened bedroom. I stayed very still and listened.

There was the eternal buffeting and moaning of the wind, there was the desultory, arrhythmic squeak of the shutter, there was the distant whistle of the electric cables. And then there was something subsonic, almost a feeling. I pulled my Sig and moved across the floor to the bedroom door. It was small, musty and dark. Like the other room, there was no mattress on the bed. The wardrobe stood open, as did the drawers in the tallboy and the bedside table. The glass in the window, and the sealed shutter, rattled quietly, like the madness outside was trying to get in.

I turned. The body was silhouetted in the arch, in the pale glow from the kitchen. It stood motionless, thin, with both hands hanging by its side. The face was invisible. My skin went cold.

I raised the pistol. "Who are you? What are you doing here?"

It didn't answer. It just stood and looked at me.

"I'm going to count to three, then things get ugly. So you'd better start talking."

I counted to two in my mind. Then the voice, quiet, low, said, "You going to shoot me?" The voice was familiar. I lowered the weapon. "That would be ironic, wouldn't it? After talking so much to Mom and Dad about protecting me."

"I didn't recognize you. You're in silhouette."

"You're in the shadows."

I stepped out of the room, out of the darkness, into the beige gloom of the living room. She remained framed in silhouette in the arch. I said, "What are you doing here, Maggie?"

"What are you doing?"

I slipped the weapon back in its holster, under my arm. "Are you always so confrontational, or is it only with people who save your parents' lives?"

"I don't trust people, Mr. Brenner. I don't believe anybody does anything for nothing."

"Does that include you? You see a lost child in a busy street, crying for her mother, what do you do? Do you walk on by or do you stop to help?"

She didn't answer. I laughed. "Oh, OK, so this is some kind of ego trip. Everybody else in the world is a bastard, but you are the one good guy. I guess that makes you pretty special, definitely a cut above the rest of us mere mortal shits."

Now she took a step and the light from the kitchen illuminated half her face.

"You know you have a real special way of giving me a pain in the ass."

"Remind me to give a damn sometime. Now, are you going to tell me why you're here or not?"

"Is there any reason why I should?"

I sighed. "I can think of a couple, Maggie. The first is that, whether you like it or not, whether you believe it or understand it or not, I am here to shut down Oz's gang. That is a good thing for you and your family."

"And the second?"

"The second is more subtle. You see, I am beginning to wonder why you are so hostile to me. Most daughters would be grateful to a man who saved her parents—and her—from the likes of Bobby and his pals. But all it seems to do for you is, in your words, give you a special kind of pain in your ass. Now I come here, and I find you here too. And I am thinking, there cannot be many people who know that Oz and his boys used to use this place. So how come you know? How come you're here? How come, Maggie, you are so pissed at the fact that I am trying to help your parents?"

She was very quiet and very serious. Finally she said, in a small voice, "And the third?"

I shook my head. "You don't want to know the third. We don't want to get there. Maggie, were you a friend of Bobby's? Have you got friends in Oz's gang?"

"No." It was emphatic, and there was hatred in her eyes.

"Then you had better start talking, or we are going to have a very big problem."

She bristled. "Are you threatening me?"

"Yes, and make no mistake, Maggie. I can and will make good on my threats."

She took a couple of steps toward me, and now I could see her face more clearly, flushed pink in the cheeks, with bright angry eyes.

"You bastard! What is it with you? *I know!*" She clenched her fists. "I know I should be grateful."

"Go see a shrink! Analyze it and work it out! But do it when this is all over! Then you can send me a message telling my why I am such an asshole. Meantime, lives are at risk, among them yours, your mother's and your father's. So why don't you cut the bullshit and tell me why the hell you are here?"

She made an inarticulate noise of frustration and turned away.

"Enough, Maggie. Talk to me." She sighed and lowered herself onto the arm of the chair. On a hunch I said, "Is it your sister?"

"That obvious, huh?"

"It's pretty obvious, yeah. What's the problem?"

"She disappeared."

I was quiet. I sat on the arm of the vinyl sofa. "How long ago?"

"A couple of months. Two or three months after the gang moved into the area."

"But your sister was in San Diego."

"Yes, but we have always been a very close-knit family, Mr. Brennan. Heather used to come up at least once a month to visit. They always had a room for her at the hotel, and she always had a room at the farm. We were close, real close."

"So what happened?"

"She came up to visit. Must have been some time in June. Late June, I think. By that time the gang had made the saloon their regular hangout when they were in town. It used to be a nice family place, and we'd go over and have a drink, catch up, gossip. So on that particular night there were like six or seven of them sitting at a table, drinking. We just ignored them and talked to each other. But after a while one of them comes over to our table. I think he was like the boss, the alpha. He was a big guy, bald, with the coldest, cruelest eyes I have ever seen, and he looked down at Heather and said, 'I like you.' Just like that. Heather tried to make light of it. I think she said something like, 'Well, thank you, that's very nice of you.' Something like that, but he just grins and says, 'No, you don't understand. I *like* you.'

"I was going to give the jerk a mouthful, but Heather just put her hand on mine and said, 'Well, that's very flattering, it's been nice, but it's late and we need to be getting home.' You know, that kind of thing. He watched us get up, grinning at us like a crazy man. His pals at the table were pissing themselves with laughter.

We left and he didn't do anything, he just watched us, and kept saying to Heather, 'I like you.' Fuckin' creep.

"Next morning she got in her car and left. And we never heard from her again. I called her several times, and left a load of messages, but she never answered. After a couple of weeks I went up to Vazquez and spoke to the sheriff. But he's a useless piece of shit and told me I should talk to the San Diego PD. So I did. I drove over to San Diego, went to her apartment, went to the hospital, but nobody had seen her since she'd come to visit us. I went to the San Diego police and reported her missing. They took down all the details, said I should talk to the sheriff and pretty much told me there was not much they could do."

"You told them about Oz?"

"That was Oz?"

"Sounds like him."

"Yeah, I told them, and they asked me if there was any evidence connecting the gang to my sister's disappearance, other than the remarks that guy made."

"So you convinced your mother that Heather was too busy to come and visit—"

"I had to protect them and I didn't know how. It would kill them if they thought something had happened to her. I told them we had spoken on the phone a couple of times. I said she was preparing for her specialization, that she promised she'd come and see us soon." She took a deep breath and sagged. "And all the while I am more and more convinced that that animal waylaid her on her way back to Cali, and she is lying dead somewhere in a shallow grave."

She covered her face and started to sob. "And what can I do? I'm not a cop, I'm not a detective, or some guy like you!" She gestured at me with an open hand. "I can't afford a private eye. So what do I do? I keep my farm working and I keep lying to my mom and dad."

She dried her eyes with the heels of her hands and wiped her nose on her sleeve. I said, "So, what *are* you doing here?"

She shrugged. "I guess I got all fired up listening to you talk. I had heard a while back, just after those bastards moved into Hope, that they'd been using this place for maybe a year or two. Nobody knew what they used it for, but the assumption was they used it to grow weed or something like that. Some people said they'd seen Arizona plates on some of the bikes and their trucks, but they came down here regular. Then one day they just upped and left, in a real hurry. The cops and the sheriff's department showed up, crawling all over the place. Then they left too, and it's been like this ever since."

"And?"

"So after a couple of beers and a shot of bourbon, I decided I was going to come down here and have a look, and see if there was anything they didn't take with them, and which the cops missed, that might tell me something about who these bastards are, and what they did to my sister."

I sat and nodded for a moment, staring at the filthy carpet under my feet. After a moment she said, "What about you? What are you doing here?"

I smiled and gave a small snort. "Pretty much the same thing. Except, obviously, I was not looking for information about your sister."

I studied her for a moment, wondering how much to tell her, how much she needed to know, how much she had a right to know. This was not an official job, so I had no guidelines. It was just me, out for murder. So I told her a little of the truth.

"This is not an official investigation, Maggie. I told you the official investigation collapsed." And then I lied a little: "I am hoping to find something that will allow for a second investigation, where the source of the evidence will be unknown to the FBI, the cops and the court, so it can't be thrown out."

"Oh." She nodded.

"But there is more to it than that, Maggie. I am going to give you the choice. I can tell you what this place was, and what I am here to do, or you can leave, take your parents to safety, and forget you ever met me and we ever had this conversation. You choose."

Her eyes were steady. "I want to know."

"This place was a film studio. These men trafficked in child pornography, and in the end they shot films here." She covered her mouth with her hands. I went on. "They got off on a technicality, and it will be very difficult to get them to face justice again because of the double jeopardy rules. And even if they did go to prison, they would probably rule the roost in there and live like kings."

Her eyes were wide, her fingers still over her mouth. "So what can you do?"

"I am going to kill them," I said. "Each and every one of them."

EIGHT

THE AIR HAD TURNED A PALE GRAY. THE WIND WAS picking up, churning the white sand into tall eddies and dragging them around the yard, draping them over the buildings and the large, red hangar. We hunched into our shoulders, leaned into the wind, and tramped across the beaten earth to the big, blue door that was rattling a soft tattoo in the blustering air. It took me about fifteen seconds to pick the padlock and we rolled the door back. The echoes rolled in, bounced off the walls and died in the shadows.

We stepped inside. Like the house, the gloom in the hangar seemed to isolate us from the battering outside. It was a huge, hollow space, with deep shadows overhead and blackness in the corners. At the far end there were what at first looked like several rooms with the near wall missing. Then, as we approached, it dawned on me that they were sets. From what I could make out, there were three bedrooms and a living room.

Against the walls either side of us there were large, plywood boards, jumbled stacks of furniture, a couple racks of clothes. I felt sick as I looked at them and thought about what they had been used for. We moved to the end and inspected the sets. They could have been sets from any sitcom. They were neutral, generic, without any kind of defining character, but as Maggie looked at them I saw tears in her eyes.

I heard myself say, "There is nothing here."

Her voice came back, small in the cavernous space.

"There has to be something."

"Everything that incriminated them was either taken by the Feds, when they blew it, or disposed of by Oz after the event."

"What were you hoping to find?"

I shook my head, scanning the vast hangar, trying to pierce the shadows.

"I don't know. It all happened real fast. The Feds broke in and took a stash of incriminating, damning evidence. What they didn't know was that Oz had caught them on CCTV camera. So at the same time that the Feds and local law enforcement were swooping in here and in Arizona, Oz's lawyers were frantically slapping injunctions on state and federal authorities, claiming the evidence had been illegally obtained and could not be used. Everything ground to a halt and all charges had to be dropped."

"But?"

I turned to face her, thinking. "But, like I said, it was a frantic rush. And Oz must have had a frantic rush too, to conceal whatever evidence the Feds had not taken, before the FBI and local law enforcement descended on them. Because during that time before the injunctions took effect, any evidence obtained under warrant, might just be admissible. So Oz didn't have a lot of time. If there was incriminating stuff here, he might just have hidden it. My boss thinks he did."

"Wouldn't they have taken it since then?"

"Not if they feared they were being watched. I was hoping, maybe, with just a little bit of luck, they might have left something concealed here."

She shuddered. "Movies?"

"Maybe, memory cards, USB devices, hard drives. He was also involved in drug trafficking, there might be a stash of drugs or cash. Anything that might have got left behind in the rush, hidden to keep it away from the authorities."

She stepped onto one of the sets and stood staring down at a bed.

"So where do you hide something like that? In a mattress?"

I smiled. "Maybe, but I don't think so. Oz is a son of a bitch, but he's smart. It would be somewhere hard to find."

"Buried." I turned to look at her. She stepped down from the set and came up close to me. "That's the obvious thing to do in this wilderness. On this plain, the sand is so fine, and there is always either a breeze or a wind, any traces of digging are gone within a few minutes."

"Where the hell would you start to look?"

"Exactly." She looked past me at the luminous square of the opening fifty paces away. "This place gives me the creeps. Do you think we should have closed the door?"

"I haven't tried the light switches," I said, with just a little irony, "but somehow I don't think the power is on."

"I guess not."

"You want to give me a hand? I'm beginning to think this was a wild goose chase, but as long as we're here we may as well scour the place."

There weren't actually that many places to look. We were essentially in a big, steel box with stacks of boards and furniture in it. You can't dig holes or lift floorboards in steel boxes, so once we had investigated beneath and behind those items, that was pretty much it.

I was debating disemboweling the mattresses and the chairs, when Maggie said, "Well, I guess we still have the sheds and the outhouses."

I smiled. "You mean before we start digging?"

The voice that answered me wasn't Maggie's. It came from the door, thirty paces away. It said, "Where are you going to dig?"

It was just a silhouette, black against the dull glow of the white sand. The squat form and the hat told me it was the sheriff, but he wasn't alone. There were four or five men behind him; a couple were just black stencils, others you could see their beards moving in the wind, and their black shades.

I didn't answer, but I took a couple of steps forward, to place myself between them and Maggie.

"You got some kind of authorization to be in this property, Mr. Brennan?"

I smiled, and let the smile show in my voice. "That's something you don't want to know about, Sheriff. If you knew the authority I have to be here, I guarantee you'd be pissing in your Levis."

There was a hint of uncertainty in his voice. Sheriff Matías Olvera was not a difficult man to shake. "What's that supposed to mean?" he asked.

I took another few steps closer to him, and now I could see the thugs he'd brought with him. There were five, Oz was not among them.

"Any of you boys have an authorization to be here?" Nobody said anything, but a couple of the bikers glanced at each other. The sheriff started to say, "I'll ask the questions..."

But I interrupted him. "How about you, Sheriff? You got some kind of warrant or permission to be on this property? As far as I am aware, your boss, Oscar Larsen, is no longer a tenant in this place."

"I don't..." He looked nervously at the men behind him. "He ain't my..."

I interrupted him again. "What you need, Sheriff, is to go back to school and learn your law. This is private property, and without a warrant you have no right to be here. Period."

His voice became a little shrill. "Well, what are *you* doin' here, then? Where's your warrant?"

I went and stood real close, looking down into his face. "I don't need one, Sheriff. I already told you that. Now, you and these monkeys here lay one finger on me or my associate, and I promise you, you will find yourself so tied up in injunctions and lawsuits you'll have to sell your soul to the devil just to pay for gas to get to the courtroom. Or maybe you already did that."

I put my hand on his chest and pushed him aside, scanning the five thugs, looking for the most dangerous one. He was standing right behind the sheriff in a denim jacket with the sleeves removed. He had black Wayfarer glasses and matted black hair and a beard.

"You go back to Oz, ape-man, and you tell him that my right to be on this property comes from the fact that I am renting it for the next year. If there is anything here he wants, he can come and ask me for it."

His voice was a low growl. "I don't have to tell Oz shit. I came here to gut you like a fish, and that's what I'm going to do."

He was surprisingly fast, and as soon as the words were out, the blade was in his right hand. He lunged at me. I felt the cold steel brush my belly and I sprang a long step back. He charged, slashing at my face, and two of his pals closed in to grab me. On my right a guy with a black bandana and on my left a blond giant with a belly that was a monument to beer.

I skipped another long step, but this time I angled toward the beer belly and let him grab my arm. He looked real pleased with himself for all of half a second, until I brought my fist pounding down onto his sixty pounds of gut, forcing it to drag down on his diaphragm, emptying his lungs and putting his heart into spasm. He went bright mauve, then deathly white as he wheezed and dropped to his knees.

Black Bandana was on me, grabbing at my right arm. I jumped in at him and brought my left forearm crashing across the crooks of his elbows, drawing him closer. He was too close for a punch so I smashed my elbow into his jaw.

That left three: Denim Jacket with the knife ahead of me, a guy with a death's head tattoo on his forehead on my right, and a guy with a black T-shirt with a baphomet on it on my left; plus the sheriff. I didn't pause to think. The three of them were coming at me. So I bounded to their left and smashed the heel of my boot into the Death's Head's knee. He staggered and fell on his back.

I didn't want to mess with Denim Jacket's knife while he had his pal the Baphomet and the sheriff for backup. Only a few seconds had passed, and I needed to finish this fast. So I feinted at denim jacket with a front kick and as my right foot landed I jumped to the left with my back foot and smashed my instep into the Baphomet's balls.

He collapsed to the floor, wheezing. Denim Jacket stopped dead, staring at me. I bent and pulled the Fairbairn and Sykes from my boot and walked toward him.

"You got some idea now what happened to Bobby and his friends?"

By the time he'd got as far as "Look, I..." the razor-sharp blade of the fighting knife had pierced his trachea and I had punched it out the side of his neck, severing the jugular and the aorta. The blood exploded from his neck and sprayed all over the sheriff. He backed away on short steps, raising his arms. Inside I heard Maggie scream, but I ignored her and, as the body crumpled to the floor, I stepped over to the sheriff, who was frantically wiping his face.

"I'm not going to kill you, Sheriff. I have a thing about not killing law enforcement officers, even if they are gutless shits like you. I can't promise that won't change, because the truth is, you're not fit to wear the badge."

I turned to Maggie. She had wide eyes and her mouth was hanging open with her fingertips on her lips.

"What you just saw was self-defense, right?" She nodded. I said, "Good. The sheriff and I are going to talk about the report he is going to make when he gets back to Vazquez. You want to go and wait in your car?"

"Yes," she said, "Yes!" and she ran.

I turned to the sheriff. "How many men has Oz got?"

He looked around. "Now?"

I shook my head, pulled the Sig from under my arm and shot

Baphomet, Death's Head, Black Bandana and the Beer-Belly in the head one after another. The sheriff's legs were trembling and I could see the dark stain on his pants. I said, "Now, how many men has he got left?"

"Twenty, or something... Look, mister, if you're CIA or something..."

"What do you do for Oz?"

"I, nothing, I just look the other way, if he needs something I help out, I..."

"What happened to Maggie's sister, Heather?"

"She, she, she...," he pressed his knees together and his face crumpled, "Oh, God! She is still with Oz, she's his...his..."

"His slave."

He made strangled, high-pitched noises. "No... It's complicated."

I narrowed my eyes and shook my head. "What made you believe that you were entitled to be a sheriff?"

He shrugged and started sobbing, with tears and saliva on his chin. "You're asking me weird questions. I don't know..."

"You're a disgrace, Matías, not just to your badge and your uniform, but to men, to humanity. I should shoot you where you stand. Go home, take a shower, resign your office. If I ever see you again with a badge, I will kill you on the spot. You understand that, don't you?"

"Yes."

"Now answer me this, and I will know if you lie. Did Oz leave something of value here? Drugs, films, money?"

He nodded slowly. "He figured you might think that. He sent these boys here to wait for you. He thinks you done something to Bobby too, and you're here to look for his stash. The Feds never found it..."

"His stash?"

"He's waiting for things to cool down before he comes and gets it. He's certain the Bureau are watching him. He says you're a Fed and you've come to steal from him."

"What is it, the stash?"

"I don't know exactly. Films, about ten Ks of coke and heroin, and a lot of money in cash."

"Where?"

"I don't know. I swear to God I don't know. He wouldn't tell me a thing like that."

"Leave. Go away, Matías. Leave Vazquez and leave New Mexico, because I swear if Oz doesn't kill you I will. Go."

He scrambled and ran. I went to the gate and watched him speed out onto the long, white road, trailing a high cloud of dust. As I turned to head back to the big hangar, I saw Maggie standing in the lee of the house, with the abandoned hogs behind her. The wind was tugging at her hair. I put the P226 away and walked to where she was standing.

"I'm sorry you had to see that."

"Was it necessary?"

"What do you think?"

She looked away. "I don't know."

"I think it was necessary. If I hadn't killed them, they would have killed us. That's what they were here for. They still might. He still has twenty or thirty men at the Farm."

She didn't answer.

"Go back to Hope, get your mother and your father and go away. Do you need money?"

Now she looked at me, eyes wide with anger and astonishment. "No!"

"Then go. Call me in a few days." I handed her my card. "I'll tell you if it's safe to come back."

She took the card slowly. Like there was something about it that was hard to believe. I ignored the look, feeling suddenly sour and bitter.

"Your sister, according to the sheriff she's still alive. I'll do my best to get her back to you in one piece."

She was frowning hard again, still shaking her head. "Who the fuck *are* you?"

I thought about how to answer a question like that, and shrugged. "A regrettable human being, trying somehow to be useful."

"*Useful?*"

"You'd better go, before you say something you'll regret."

"What are you going to do?"

I looked toward the hangar. "I need to hide some bikes and bury some trash."

"Jesus!" She turned and started trudging across the open ground, with the dust and the wind battering her from behind. It snatched her words from her mouth and flung them in the air, but I still heard them. "What an asshole," she said to herself. "Come on, we did this together, I'll help you bury them. There must be spades in the sheds, otherwise you're going to be digging with your damned hands."

I watched her walk away, smiled to myself and followed.

NINE

It was as she was rummaging through one of the sheds that an idea came into my head. It was a brutal, barbaric idea and it made me smile.

"It's OK," I said suddenly, speaking above the moans and rattles outside. "We won't bury them. I have a better idea. Help me load them into the back of my Jeep."

She dropped a big tin of Ready Seal against a couple of old wooden posts and stared at me, squinting.

"What?"

"Digging a hole big enough for these guys is going to take more time than we can afford, especially if we want them deep enough that bits won't be dragged all over New Mexico and Texas by random wildlife. Besides, I have a quicker, more efficient way of disposing of them. Trust me."

"Yeah, I do. That's what worries me. So what do you want to do?"

"Help me get them in the back of the Jeep. We'll leave the Jeep here, in the hangar with the bikes. Then we go collect your parents and take them to your ranch. You get the hell out of here and, just in case, you do not tell me where you are going."

She didn't look happy. She stared at my chest like a child who's been told she can't have her candy.

"What are you going to do?"

I shook my head. "Where I'm going you can't follow. What I've got to do you can't be any part of, Maggie."

"Yeah, that's funny. Hysterical."

"I'm serious. It's best all round if you don't know. It reduces the risk for both of us—for all of us."

"So..." She shrugged. "What...?"

"Call me on my cell in a couple of days."

"That's great." She slammed the shed closed and stormed away toward the hangar.

It was a difficult and unpleasant job lifting the five bodies into the back of the Jeep, but Maggie was strong and between us we eventually managed it. When we'd shoved the last one in she slammed the door closed and leaned her back against the truck.

"Is this what a first date is like with you? If you like a girl, you go out together, kill a few guys, scare the bejaysus out of her, and if she survives, you take her out for a drink, or dinner?"

I repressed a smile. "Who says I like you?"

She arched an eyebrow and I followed her out, where we brought the bikes inside and parked them along one wall. Then we slammed the big, blue sliding door of the hangar shut and fitted the padlock. Finally, we made our way to her red Toyota. It was as we were climbing in that she paused, pointed at my belly and frowned. "What the hell is that?"

My shirt was torn, and there was a big stain.

"Yeah," I said. "It's beginning to bother me. You any good at first aid? It's just a flesh wound, but it might need stitches."

She slammed the door and fired up the engine. As we came out of the gate she turned left, west, toward Dell City, instead of right toward the Guadalupe and Hope.

"What are you doing? We need to get your parents."

"No." She shook her head. "Don't get me wrong. I am not going to start mouthing off, complaining about macho shit.

When you wrestle steers, and work this damned desert every day just to make ends meet, let me tell you you're grateful for a few guys who are full of macho shit. All that 'strong woman' feminist bull is a luxury those East Coast and California academics can allow themselves. But when I get up at four in the morning to go and feed the cattle, I do not want a couple of boys with me who are in touch with their feminine side mincing through the shit and takin' time off to put fuckin' moisturizer on their hands."

She went quiet for a moment, then shrugged. "I lost track of what I was saying. Point is, you're tough. You know—" She let go of the wheel with her right hand and waved it at the gash in my belly. "You weren't whining about how you'd been cut. That's good. A guy should be tough, but—oh, yeah," she glanced at me and nodded, "I remember now, before we go and get Mom and Dad, I am going to fix your belly." She raised her hand. "Don't argue. Oz does not even know yet that his boys are not coming back. We saved time by not burying them. And if you show up at the hotel like that, Mom is going to have a fit. I clean you up and then we go and get Mom and Dad."

I sighed. I was feeling tired and my belly was starting to hurt. What she was saying was probably right, and the truth was I could not afford an infected wound right now.

"Fine," I said. "But be quick. We do it quick."

"And another thing," she said, ignoring my comment. She grinned and wagged her finger at me. "Don't you tell me you don't like me, because I seen the way you look at my legs."

"What?"

"I seen it." She chuckled and smiled at the long, white dusty road ahead. I sighed and closed my eyes, suppressing a smile. People react to shock in many ways, often by making wildly inappropriate jokes at totally inappropriate times. But the fact was, I had to admit, she did have, as she would say, a pair of mighty fine legs.

We followed the road out of the sand flats and in among the fields that surround Dell City. Eventually we turned right onto

Main Street. You'd be forgiven for not realizing you were in a town at all. There were low, scattered buildings anything from thirty to a hundred and thirty yards apart. Main Street was black-top, and so was Broadway, which intersected it, but the rest were all dirt roads. I didn't see a single traffic light or a store as we drove through.

Pretty soon we'd left the town behind us and a couple of miles north she slowed and turned in through a gate on the left. We rattled down the track and came to a big, stone house with a gabled roof and a big yard on the left. There were a handful of outhouses and sheds, and what looked like a new, wooden prefab that might have been sleeping accommodation.

"I have a couple of hands who sleep over in the quarters yonder. We don't socialize and they know to respect me. They get the work done. Then there's Maria who helps around the house." She pulled up and killed the engine. "C'mon, let's get you patched up."

We climbed out. It hurt, but I could walk just fine. However, when she put her arm around my waist and my arm around her shoulders, I didn't complain. She led me down the side of the house and through a kitchen door. There was a woman in there I figured was Maria. She was in her late fifties or early sixties, rotund, with hair that was largely still black pulled back in a bun. She put a large knife and an onion to her head as we came in and said, "*Ay! Dios mío!*"

"It's no big deal, Maria," said Maggie on my behalf. "It's just a cut. Get hot water, soap, antiseptic cream, bandage and a roll of sticking plaster. Got that?"

She sat me at the big, rough wooden table and Maria said, "*Que?*"

Maggie repeated the whole thing in Spanish and then took off my shirt. It was just a cut, but it was an ugly cut, about a quarter of an inch deep, right into the muscle and it was bleeding a lot. I said, "It'll need stitches. Can you do that?"

After a moment she said, "No. I guess. Maybe." And then, "When is this going to stop?"

"I'm sorry." I tried to smile. "Soon, I promise."

"I didn't mean that."

"OK, look, we'll do this together. I need to be standing up or lying down, all right? And you need to keep it as clean and as dry as possible. But first we have to wash the wound."

She nodded and swallowed, then swallowed again. "Just, ordinary needle and thread?"

"That will do fine."

"What color?"

I raised an eyebrow. She gave a single, nervous giggle and went to get the needle and thread.

She and Maria returned together, muttering to each other in Spanish. They dumped the bits on the table and Maria went to get hot water.

Washing an open knife wound hurts, and there's not a lot you can do about that, unless you happen to have an anesthesiologist handy. I didn't have one of those so all I could do was grunt and puff and occasionally blaspheme, to which Maria would make Mother Hen noises like, "Hoy, hoy, hoy..." and click her tongue.

When it was clean I stood and between them they tried to keep it dry while I sewed the gash with white cotton and a sewing needle dowsed in surgical spirits. It is not hard to describe the pain. It's impossible. So the chances are I made do with four stitches where five would have been better. By the time I'd done four, number five was just not going to happen.

After that Maggie smothered the mess I had made with antiseptic cream, covered it in gauze and then laid strips of sticking plaster across it. She followed that with a bandage wrapped around my waist.

"What I need now," I told Maggie, "is four aspirins and a large glass of whisky, no ice."

She said something to Maria in Spanish and Maria left the

room, clucking and shaking her head again. Maggie went to the fridge and poured me a large glass of milk.

"You're too young to get an ulcer," she said.

I was pretty sure there was some wiseass rejoinder I should be able to come back with, but all my brain could think about was the pain in my belly, so I nodded, took the glass and drained it. When I handed it back I was surprised to see tears in her eyes. She snatched the glass away and took it to the sink.

Maria came in with a pack of aspirin and a moderate glass of bourbon. She wagged her finger at me as I took them. "No good! No good for you!"

I attempted a smile. "Yes, thank you, *gracias.*"

She watched me with the kind of severity only mothers know how to produce as I downed the pills and took a good pull on the drink. Maggie, who had been leaning on the sink staring out at the yard, took Maria and led her out of the room. I closed my eyes and listened to the low, urgent monologue, punctuated by gasps and tuts from Maria. Shortly after that the front door opened and closed, and Maggie returned to the kitchen.

"You're used to this. I'm completely lost. I am all at sea. I don't know what I'm doing or feeling. One minute I think I'm going nuts, then I'm in a panic, then for God's sake I start *flirting* with you! Next I am terrified for my parents, then I see those men going down one after another."

"Believe me," I said with my eyes still closed. "You never get used to it."

"How," she said, "How could we, in the truck coming back, how could we joke, and *flirt!* And act like, like nothing had happened, and you had just killed five men! And we, and we, and we...."

I opened them to look at her. She went rigid and I stood and put my arms around her. At first her arms stayed stiff by her sides, then she gripped me with her wrists and finally flung her arms around me and squeezed. The pain was indescribable, but I couldn't bring myself to tell her. Instead I spoke softly in her ear.

"Don't beat yourself up, Maggie. You haven't killed anybody. And shock affects people in weird ways. Joking and flirting is one way of coping. Your brain is just trying to kid you into believing everything is normal. The best thing you can do is go with it, and don't beat yourself up."

I could feel her wet tears on my chest. After a while her breathing began to settle.

"You're just saying that," she said, and I felt her hand move up my back to wipe her face and her nose awkwardly across my arm, "because you want me to keep flirting with you."

I stood back and held her at arm's length. "That transparent, huh? Well, OK, the flirting bit I made up. But the rest of it's true."

She stepped a little closer, frowning up into my eyes. I realized suddenly how mobile her face was. A thousand tiny expressions flitted across it among the wincing of her eyebrows and the twitching corners of her mouth. "Does it hurt?" she asked, touching the bandage gently with her fingers.

"Yes, like hell, but it's easing off."

"Does it hurt if I do this?"

She pressed herself against me, with her arms encircling me and her head against my chest.

"Not as much as you might think."

She looked up into my face and smiled. "You're insane," she whispered. And then, standing on tiptoe, "I'm going with it, like you advised. So take me upstairs and show me some of your macho bullshit."

It is my job to take out very bad people. That is my job. But that does not mean that I am full of moral rectitude and always make enlightened decisions. In fact, I very rarely think, "This is wrong, I should not do it." I am far more likely to think, "I may never have this opportunity again, I should seize the moment."

Somewhat less elegantly put, that was what I thought as Maggie's mouth closed on mine. What happened after that was between Maggie, the bedposts and me.

. . .

A COUPLE of hours later we made our way North along the 1437, which was basically Main Street Dell City, extended north between huge fields. It eventually intersected with the G003 going northeast, and the 506 going east, and that was the route we took. There was less wind up there than down among the White Sands Flats, where the Guadalupe River wound through the vast dust bowl, and Maggie opened the windows to let the clean, desert air in. We didn't talk until we had veered a little north into the desert, leaving the flat fields behind us, rattling and grinding through the wilderness of small, gnarled shrubs and yucca. The wind had dropped, but heavy, inky-blue clouds were lowering in the southeast, creeping in from the Gulf. I wondered if there would be a storm, and if so, how it would affect things.

"I don't do that," Maggie said suddenly.

I pulled my mind from the possibility of storms and floods and frowned at her.

"What's that?"

"Jump into bed with a guy just because, you know, I like him."

For the second time I couldn't think of a wiseass rejoinder, so I just said, "I know you don't."

She turned from the wheel and gave me a very direct stare. "'Cause you could get the wrong idea. And I *do not* want you to get the wrong idea. You know when the last time was that I had physical relations with a man?"

"About twenty minutes ago."

She ignored the wisecrack and plowed on. "I had the same boyfriend from the time I was twenty until two years ago. I broke up with him and I have not been with a man since. Until now."

I didn't know what to say, and the effect of the whiskey and the aspirins was wearing off, being replaced by stiletto stabs in my belly. I didn't say anything. I just looked at her and did things with my eyebrows.

"You're the first," she added. "In all that time. So don't go thinkin' that I'd do that with just anybody."

"I wouldn't think that, and I am," I couldn't think of the right word so I mumbled something like, "honored."

"Don't patronize me, Harry. I know I am in uncharted water here, and I don't need to be mollycoddled. I just need *you* to know who *I* am."

"OK, I know who you are. I knew anyway, but now I really know."

"OK."

We eventually wound and twisted our way onto the Hope Road and, half an hour later, we ground to a halt outside the hotel, to be enveloped by the cloud of dust we'd been trailing for the last twelve miles. We climbed out of the truck and she ran up the stairs ahead of me as I hobbled behind. When I finally got to the top and pushed through the doors the three of them were standing, holding each other and looking at me. So I scowled at them.

"What?"

It was Bill who answered. He said, "We're not going."

TEN

I stood shaking my head.

"No," I said, "no, do not do this. It is absolutely out of the question. You," I pointed at Maggie, "get your parents' bags, put them in their car, leave me the truck, and get the hell out of here. Call me the day after tomorrow."

Bill drew breath and took a step forward. I didn't even let him get started. I raised a hand. "I am grateful, Bill. Truly I am. You're a good, very courageous man, but we cannot put your wife and daughter at risk. You need to be there to protect them. And besides," I lied, "I know exactly how I am going to handle these guys. I don't need backup. You—" I pointed at Maggie again. Her mouth was a thin line and there were tears in her eyes. "Get your parents out of here!"

She knew ultimately that I was right and that she actually had no choice. She gently propelled her mother toward the door. "Come on, Mom." Her mother went, looking down at the floor, and Bill, after giving me a resentful look, followed after them.

After they'd gone I leaned on the reception counter for a moment, waiting for the pain in my belly to subside. Feet running up the steps outside made me look. Maggie pushed through the door. She went behind the reception desk and handed me a bunch of keys.

"These are the keys to the hotel. Mom called the woman who takes care of the cleaning. She'll look after things while we're gone." She stared at me. "You need help. You can't do this alone."

"Believe me, Maggie, the best help you can give me is to keep your mom and dad safe."

She reached in her pocket and pulled out the keys to the old Toyota. Without warning she recited a number. Then said, "I'm switching off the GPS on my phone and my parents'. Nobody can trace us. But the minute this is over you call me. I'm going to be thinking about you every minute of every day. You hear?"

I nodded. "I hear."

She came round the counter, flung her arms around me, kissed me and stormed out. A moment later I heard the whine of an engine recede into the sultry afternoon.

When it was gone I went behind the counter and found the first-aid kit. I opened it, took a handful of aspirins and threw them in my mouth. Then I made my way to the kitchen, through the dining room, and washed them down with two glasses of water. After that I went up to my room.

Under the bed was the military kit bag I had brought with me the day I'd arrived. I dragged it out, unzipped it and pulled out a Heckler and Koch with a mounted GLM. In the bag were a stash of spare magazines, night-vision goggles and four cakes of C4 with cell phone-compatible detonators.

I carried it down to the Toyota and slung it in the back. Then I went inside again, back to the kitchen, and ate a couple of burgers. After that I lay down and rested for a couple of hours.

At four thirty I rose, had a cold shower, dressed and went down to the Toyota. I climbed behind the wheel and drove back to the studio. There I left Maggie's truck in the hangar, switched my kit bag to the Jeep. I took a couple of minutes to plug a detonator into a one-pound cake of C4 and set it on my cell to the number nine. Finally, at six PM, as the dark started closing in, I headed north, toward Vazquez.

The sky in the west was on fire, and smoldering embers lay in two long arms around the horizon. All around me the desert was sinking into shadows, where shrubs and gnarled trees rose like the silhouettes of dying fingers reaching out of the dead soil. Here and there, silent, invisible predators began to emerge, listening, smelling, waiting.

After about ten minutes I spotted the floodlit glow of Oz's compound. I made no effort to conceal my presence. On the contrary, I drove around to the track that led from the road to the main gate. I didn't see many people outside: just three dogs and a couple of guys who watched me pass.

I nosed into the drive, drove up to the gate and turned the truck around, facing the road with its ass to the farm. I dumped a pound of C4 at the gate and wrenched open the back of the Jeep. Then I started hauling out the bodies. It hurt my belly like hell, and I felt the warm trickle of blood where the stitches had torn with the effort. But by the time I'd dragged the last body out and swung back into the cab, I could see some guys approaching from the farmhouse in a Dodge RAM. So it had been worth it.

I put the Jeep in gear and accelerated to the end of the drive. There I stopped, snatched the Heckler and Koch from the back seat and looked through the rear window. Two guys had climbed out of the RAM and had opened the gates. Now they were just standing staring down at their dead pals and occasionally looking up at the Jeep with "what the hell" faces.

I'd hoped there'd be more of them. It was a waste of C4, but at least I had the gate open, and it's a good principle to proceed as planned as long as it is possible. I pressed nine on my keypad, there was a loud, jarring smack in the air and the two guys and their five dead friends became dog food.

I put the Jeep in reverse and floored the pedal. It whined like a wasp on speed and I splatted backward through the carnage, spun the wheel, avoided the RAM and turned the nose toward the main building, then hurtled forward, burning rubber around the drive toward the back of the house, where I 'd seen the dish aerial and the men laboring.

When I got there, there were guys spilling out of the back door. I slammed on the brakes, took half a second to aim through my near window and let off two controlled bursts and lobbed two grenades at them. Then I floored the gas, fishtailed so the body of the truck was between me and the cowering, scattering men and swung down from the cab. I peered through the rear window and saw there were ten of them, running at me and screaming some kind of war cry. They were maybe thirty paces away. Two more were lying, dismembered in the dirt. I yanked open the door, took aim and let off four more short bursts. I heard a scream and by the time they had returned fire I was ducking behind the hood, dragging my kit bag with me. Two more short bursts in their flank took down another two guys. The whole charging mass skidded and staggered to a halt and turned to face me. Now they were ten paces away and they were charging, but there were just seven of them.

According to Claude Cockburn, running backward was a special technique developed by the Italians during the Second World War. Fact is, it can be a useful tactic, and I employed it now, putting the Jeep between me and them, running backward, firing short bursts and lobbing two more grenades.

As they detonated, one at either end of the Jeep, I dropped to my belly and rammed in a new magazine. But they didn't come spilling around the sides of the Jeep. There were just five of them left, and what they did was to take up positions using the Jeep as cover. That wasn't real bright.

I dropped a grenade under the Jeep's fuel tank and the big, beautiful beast leapt three feet into the air, belching a great ball of fire from its belly. There was a lot of screaming then. Three men thrashed and rolled in the cold desert sand, trying to beat out the flames. I shot each one in the head and set off at a run after the other two who were making for the house.

With their motivation and my belly, I knew I wasn't going to catch them. So I dropped to one knee, aimed below their hips and again let off three short bursts: nine pellets of molten lead that tore at their legs and brought them to the ground. Then I went after them at a steady lope, thinking that I had not seen Oz among them.

There are few things in this life as agonizing to watch as a man crying through fear and pain. They were both lying, face down, maybe seven feet apart. The one closest the house was half turned, with his left hand raised like he was trying to ward me off.

I asked him, "Where's Oz?"

He made inarticulate noises. I shot him through the temple and turned to the other guy who was a couple of feet away from me. "Where's Oz?"

"He ain't here."

I nodded. "That's why I'm asking you where he is."

"He took half the boys and went to the studio."

I hunkered down and frowned at him. His left leg was badly damaged and was spilling blood like an overturned bottle. His artery was torn and he probably had five minutes at most. I said, "The studio? Outside Dell City? I was there today. That place is empty."

He shook his head. "No man, not that one. I know where you went. But you gotta help me." He was having trouble breathing. "I can help you. You help me, I help you, right?"

"Sure. I'm interested in what you're telling me. Keep talking, I'll get you to a hospital. Did Heather go with him."

He smiled. "Yeah. She goes everywhere. Thanks, pal. I need a doc, real bad. I don't feel so good."

"Hang in there. What's your name?"

"Ben."

"What studio did Oz go to, Ben?"

He pointed and gave a choking laugh. "You were at the old studio, on the old Hope Road, with the girl. But Oz was at Studio Four. The new studio. Nobody knows where that is, man."

"But you do, right?"

"I do. I can take you there."

I shook my head. "You, my friend, are going to hospital. You're in bad shape." I tapped at my cell like I was dialing. "You tell me where it is, and I'll get you a doctor."

"I'm real thirsty. Give me a cold one, will you? A cold..."

"Where is the studio, Ben?"

His eyes glazed and he died.

I sat and stared at him for a while. He was staring back at me, but his eyes weren't seeing anything. He had died on a lie. Not his but mine. I had come to kill him because he was evil. But he had died asking for a small mercy, and I had lied to him as he died. Evil is not what you are, but what you do.

I put the thought out of my mind and walked into the house by the rear door.

I was in a filthy kitchen. The smell of cannabis was strong. There were mugs of cold coffee stashed beside the sink. The surfaces were littered with beer bottles and fast-food containers. In one wall there was a small door I figured led to the cellar. I stayed very still, listening. Sometimes, if you relax and focus your attention, you can detect sounds that are subsonic. They are like a disturbance in the air. And right then, as I stood in the kitchen, it was as though I could hear the breathing.

I slung the assault rifle over my shoulder and pulled the P226 from my holster. I inched across the kitchen with irregular, sliding steps until I got to the door. It was ajar. I took a firm hold of it and yanked. It gave a small squeak. I remained motionless, looking down a long, gloomy passage toward a front door with four frosted glass panels in it. Through them the ugly glare of the spotlights outside filtered in as a depressing orange glow. The smell of cannabis was stronger here.

On my left a wooden staircase rose from the front door to the upper floors. On my right there were two doors. I figured one led to a living room and the other to what would once have been a dining room. Today it would probably be Oz's den or control room, or whatever it was he had.

The noise I was sensing was in the living room. It was the sound of fear, of somebody trying not to breathe. I put the Sig in my left hand, reached across the door and in a single, rapid movement, pressed down on the handle, shoved the door open and turned, training my weapon on the opening.

There was nobody there and nothing happened. I stepped into the opening with the semiautomatic held out in front of me in both hands. Now I could hear whimpering and sobbing. It didn't make me any less careful. A whimpering, sobbing person is just as liable to blow your brains out of your head as a deadly silent one.

I moved around the door. There was a collective scream. I don't know what I had expected. Maybe I had half-expected to see Heather, or Oz. What I did see should not have surprised me, but it did. There were twelve of them. Six sitting on the sofa hugging each other, four on the floor, clinging to the legs of those on the sofa, and two more holding on to each other in a big easy chair beside the sofa: twelve girls in various stages of undress.

There was a coffee table and on it was all the paraphernalia for smoking marijuana, including those oddly depressing pieces of scrunched, singed tinfoil. There were also a couple of mirrors and a black AMEX dusted with white powder.

I sighed. Naturally they would not have set themselves up here without women. I put the Sig back in my holster and raised my right hand.

"OK, relax, I am not going to hurt you."

There was a slight lessening of tension, but they didn't look real convinced. I leaned my back against the wall. This was a hell of a mess, and one I should have foreseen. I needed these women out of this house, and silenced.

"There must be some vehicles left in this place. Where are they?"

They stared at me a moment, twelve blank faces, twelve slightly sagging mouths, twenty-four frowning eyebrows.

Then suddenly they were all talking at the same time. I pointed at the girl sitting at the center of the sofa, a blonde who was probably closer to thirty than she was to twenty.

"You," I said, "are you mother hen here?" She scowled, but several heads thought about it and then nodded. I went on. "You talk, the rest of you don't talk. We need at least one truck. Are there any trucks here on the Farm right now?"

She nodded a couple of times, slowly. I growled, "Pick up the pace, Lulu, we're on the clock."

"They took three trucks—"

"Who took three trucks?"

"Oz and the boys. They took three trucks. That means there's another three," she pointed at the wall, "in the garage. Out the side of the house."

"Where are the keys?"

"In the kitchen?"

"Are you telling me or asking me?"

She swallowed. "Don't get mad, mister. I'm trying to help. They always keep the keys in the kitchen."

"OK, now here's the million-dollar question. Stash, dope and money. Where?"

Nobody said anything, but there was a lot of eye-shifting. I sighed and pointed back toward the kitchen. "There are twelve dead men out there. Nobody is going to come in and tan your hides for talking to me, but there might be a big bonus for you girls if you help me out here."

A few of those shifting eyes lit up and Momma Hen said, "In the den next door. That's where he keeps everything. His cash and his stash."

"OK," I said, "let's go."

ELEVEN

Oz's den was pretty much what you would expect from an old, remote New Mexico farmhouse. It was large, with a wooden floor and a high ceiling. It had a bow window over on the left, and on the right there was a large, L-shaped desk with a big, black leather chair behind it and a big computer in front. And beyond that, up against the wall, there was a steel safe, four foot high, three foot deep and three foot across. It was the kind of safe that made you want what was inside it.

I looked at Mother Hen. "What's your name?"

"Xena."

"OK, Xena, there is a cash reward tonight for everyone who does as she's told. I want every functioning truck parked outside the kitchen door, with the engine running, in five minutes. I am going to go and get the key to this piggy bank. When I get back I want to see trucks parked and idling, and everybody right back in here waiting. If we all play our part, everybody goes home a little richer. Are we clear?"

She nodded and they all nodded. I said, "OK, see to it."

I went out through the kitchen door again and crossed the eerie, floodlit yard to where the Jeep was sitting, smoldering among dead, mutilated bodies. Ten paces beyond it I found my kit bag. It was almost empty, but what it contained was essential. I slung it over my shoulder and made my way back toward the house. There I saw four half-naked girls climbing daintily down from a couple of Range Rovers. It was a rare moment when I was grateful for the job karma had given me. As I came up, one of the girls asked me breathlessly, "You want we should get the RAM from the gate?"

I shook my head. "No, I'll take care of that one."

They followed me to the den and I dumped my kit bag on the desk. From it I took one of the cakes of C4 and tore off a strip. I molded it carefully into the crack of the door all the way around, placing a little extra where the hinges were, and pressed in one of the detonators.

"OK, ladies, everybody out."

The twelve girls hurried out, doing that weird thing naked women do when they run, holding their arms up like chicken wings. I followed them out, took cover and dialed nine. There was a loud bang and a ghost of smoke crept out of the door. We went back inside and there was the satisfying sight of the safe door lying on the wooden floorboards, and inside the safe a pile of cash that was so big it was hard to estimate. However much it was, it was a lot of money.

I turned to the twelve awe-struck faces in a chorus behind me. Xena was smiling with a golden light in her eyes. I suspected she had just fallen in love with me.

I said, "Where's the dope?"

"Oh," she said, unable to pull her eyes away from the safe. "That might be in the basement."

"OK, where is Studio Four?"

That made her turn and look at me. For a moment she didn't say anything. Then, uncomfortably, "It's about six miles east from here. There's no road."

"No road?"

"You come to the end of the Hope Road, where it turns south toward Hope? But you keep going straight, toward the Big Ridge.

There's a valley up, dead ahead. You'll see where the ground is scored by the rains, when the water comes down out of the canyons. You just keep goin'. Soon enough you're gonna find yourself in a big kind of basin? With big hills and canyons all around you? Well then you keep on goin' straight to the end, and on your left you're gonna see a deep canyon with a big stack of rocks near the mouth, all piled up on top of each other. You turn in there, and you follow it all around in a big bend. It's like a dry riverbed." She paused. "You're gonna see it, up on the side of the ravine. It's all made of rock and camouflaged so they won't see it with the satellites and shit, but when you're down there you can't miss it. It looks like fuckin' evil made into a hut."

I felt a hot pellet of anger smoldering in my gut as I asked her, "What do they film out there? Have any of you been?"

"Uh-huh, I went once, and Sheryl. They had a party and they wanted some girls. But mostly we just entertain 'em here. We get paid and we go home. We don't make the movies."

"One more question. What about Heather?"

They all looked at each other, then Xena shrugged. "Heather's Oz's chick. She never talks to nobody. She stoned out of her mind most of the time. She's with him now. They went to make some movies."

The kit bag was now empty, so I took the cash and stuffed it inside. They all watched me do it with anxious eyes, wondering what their share would be. When I was done I said, "I was going to blow this place tonight. I didn't know you were here. You would all have died. On your way out, have a look at the dead men who are littering the yard outside."

I paused and closed my eyes a moment, fighting off the growing weariness and the pain. I opened my eyes again and said:

"This money gets divided twelve ways equally. If anybody cheats, I'll know about it. And, ladies, once you have the cash, try to make some smart choices, OK?"

They all nodded in unison. I shoved the kit bag at them and said, "Get the hell out of here, never come back and never talk about what happened here tonight. Nobody would believe you anyway."

They grabbed the bag and ran, with weird up and down movements of their feet and their hands held up by their chests, all squealing as they went.

I watched the two Range Rovers pull away around the house and disappear in the direction of the gate. Then I made my way toward the garage, watching my shadow stretch long before me under the dead spotlights.

It was as I had figured. These had been stables and barns, and had been converted into makeshift housing for trucks and bikes. Oz and his boys had gone in three trucks – that meant some twelve or fifteen men—and they had left twelve guys behind to watch the Farm. That made up the twenty-five to thirty estimate the sheriff had given me. I heaved open the main doors and saw a mass of bikes. I took a moment to count them. There were twenty-five of them.

As you'd expect on a farm, with the nearest gas station miles away in Vazquez, there were twelve drums of gas stashed along the wall to the right of the bikes. Four of them were diesel. The other eight were gasoline. I dragged one over beside the bikes, and rolled two more over to the house. I manhandled them through the door and then opened the door to the basement. That was where Xena had said the dope would be, and she wasn't wrong.

It was stashed neatly along the back wall. There must have been twenty Ks of the stuff, forty-four pounds. I didn't bother to see if it was coke or heroin. Maybe it was both. I didn't give a damn. I was more interested in the four propane canisters that were stored down there too. They were heavy, but I carried them up to the kitchen and stashed them around one of the gasoline drums.

I stopped then for a rest. I was bone tired and my belly was hurting like hell. I found a cold beer in the fridge and drained it. I was nearly done. I just had a couple of things left to do before I headed for the Big Ridge.

I had just over two and a half pounds of C4 left. I took half a pound and carried it back to the garage, where I placed a quarter onto the gasoline drum and stuffed a detonator in it. Then I went back to the kitchen and rolled one of the two drums to the top of the cellar stairs. There I opened it and tipped it over, so it started spilling its contents down into the vault.

I put the remaining quarter pound of C4 onto the other drum, the one I had positioned beside the propane bottles, and stuck in another detonator. Then I walked out of the house and headed for the big Dodge RAM out by the gate. I pulled myself in behind the wheel. The key was still in the ignition. It roared to life and I drove out, over the trampled mess of bodies, and turned east, toward the Big Ridge mountains, and Studio Four. In my gut I knew that Oz knew I was coming for him, and he would be ready and waiting.

I took my cell from my pocket and dialed nine. The air shook, but I didn't look back. My rearview mirror filled with fire and the cab was flooded with flickering orange light as the C4 ignited the gasoline and ruptured the propane canisters. The house shuddered and expanded, then collapsed in on itself, and beside the churning inferno, the wooden stables were consumed, engulfed in fire, as the gas tanks ignited one after another in an explosive chain reaction.

I drove on into the night, toward the dark ridge that darkened the horizon, black against the translucent sky. The great fireball rose into the air behind me, churning black and red and yellow, dropping beneath it the smoldering embers of what had been Oz's Farm.

Now it was the Farm of the Dead, the cattle were all mutilated and the chickens had all run. Now there was only scorched earth and dismembered bodies: Harry's expert handiwork.

The pain throbbed at the center of my being and I realized suddenly I was becoming delirious. The black desert and the huge, looming wall of the mountains moved toward me, rattling the truck as it rolled over the rutted, pitted sand. It struck me that the sky was such a cool, deep blue you could probably drink it, and the stars, like shards of ice, would keep it cold and fresh.

A voice in my head told me I was becoming dehydrated, and I wondered whose voice it might be. Probably the colonel's, I figured.

I should stop.

I knew I should stop and go back to the hotel. I knew I needed rest and probably antibiotics. But I could not stop the desert rolling toward me, and in any case, I knew that if I did, Oz would get away. Oz always got away, like the song said. The shroud tailor measured him for a six-deep holiday, the stiff was froze and the case was closed, on the one that got away.

I had stopped. Time had passed timelessly. I didn't know how long, but I was in a huge bowl, with mountains rising all around me. The mountains were black but the sky was a transparent, dark blue, pierced by stars, and over the black ink of the ridge, the moon hung like a spotlight, flooding the plateau.

I climbed down from the truck and stared. The icy air chilled my skin and made me shudder. Rocks, I told myself, I was looking for rocks. I turned in a circle, and everything seemed impossibly far away. How could I see a pile of rocks in this endless wasteland? I clambered back into the RAM.

The engine growled and the gullies, made by years of floodwaters, now seemed to shine a pale, luminous blue in the moonlight. They were moon-paths, and I allowed them to draw me on, like silver threads pulling me home. Gradually the far end of the plateau began to rise up, closer. A black wall blocking my way, but those silver paths bent to my left before they got there. I followed, turning left also, and suddenly, there beside the luminous white strand, was a cairn, about three foot high and a couple of feet across.

Stones.

I found myself laughing, leaning on the steering wheel. I was shivering with cold, but aware that the sweat was running off my body, soaking my shirt. I had fever and dehydration. Business as usual, then.

What had she said? After the pile of rocks, follow the track, like a dry riverbed, and I would find it. Find Studio Four.

I killed the lights and let the truck roll slowly along the path as it curled gradually to the right. The sides of the canyon closed in and were steep here, cutting out the light of the moon. The path spiraled tighter, and as I came around the final bend, the steep wall on my right fell back suddenly, opening up and allowing the light of the moon to fall on the bare, gray rock face. And there, about halfway up the hill, I saw the stygian hulk of a rambling, amorphous structure.

I stopped the truck and sat for a while, I had no idea how long, shivering and sweating. I had my Sig under my arm, I had the Fairbairn and Sykes in my boot. I had the Heckler and Koch, and the grenade launcher. I had also four magazines and maybe half a dozen grenades, plus two pounds of C4 left.

I was very aware that what I didn't have left was strength. I knew I would probably fail and die that night. I could feel that real close. But I was also aware that if I did not kill Oz tonight, I would probably never kill him. And he must die, even if I died with him.

I swung down from the cab and began to laugh softly to myself. About my only regret was that I was going to die without ever having taken the colonel to bed. It was a shame she didn't know that. She'd flush, her cheeks would turn a pretty pink, she'd get cross, say something about it being inappropriate.

I slung the assault rifle over my shoulder, tucked the two cakes of C4 into my shirt and stumbled to the front of the truck.

"You've got all this hardware, Harry," I told myself, "but the one thing you haven't got, old friend, is a plan."

I scanned the side of the hill. There was some kind of a towpath that wound up the side of the ravine. I began to follow it, instinctively staying low to avoid making a silhouette against the sky. As I went I continued to talk to myself, quietly.

"You have no intel. You don't know who's in there. You know Oz is in there, and Heather, and maybe twelve men, but aside from that, pal, you don't know shit. There may be kids, maybe their parents. It's like back at the Farm, you come in, guns blazing, and there are twelve girls there, whom you could have killed, Harry. It's not good enough."

The words lingered as I trudged on, following the ink-man shadow that walked ahead of me on the luminous path.

Not good enough.

It was not good enough.

I was not good enough.

I stood thirty or forty paces from what looked like an arched opening in a pile of rocks. Yellow-amber light was filtering through the arch here and there. I wondered if they had cameras on me. A fierce stab of pain made me double over. I hunkered down and waited for it to pass, then got to my feet again and half staggered the thirty paces to the archway.

Up close I could make out it was a kind of artificial cave-cum-porch, and inside that was a heavy, arched wooden door. It was locked. It was not hard to pick, and after a few seconds it swung open. There was silence, nothing happened. I pulled the Heckler and Koch from my shoulder and eased the door open with the barrel.

In front of me I saw a tunnel, about seven foot high and six feet across. Two bare bulbs hung from the ceiling, casting a soul-destroying, suicidal light against the concrete walls. I scanned for cameras or any kind of booby-trap, but I saw nothing, except another door at the far end, maybe twenty feet away, which was also closed.

Hearing my own breathing loud in my ears I walked the distance to the second door, took hold of the handle, turned and pushed. The door swung open.

TWELVE

It looked like the inside of a prefab, like a miniature version of the hangar at the studio. Only in this one I was entering from the side and the room, maybe twelve or fifteen paces across, stretched out on either side of me. The walls, the floor and the ceiling seemed to be of steel. I stepped inside, trying to understand what I was seeing.

Across the room, eighteen or twenty feet away, there was a large square of cheap carpet. On it there was a sofa pushed against the wall, and on the sofa was a coil of thin rope. Light came from a couple of spotlights either side. I looked over to my left. In the far corner there was another door. This one was closed. Beside it there was another spotlight, and against the wall there was a board with a rough painting of a dark street with a nineteenth-century streetlamp, its amber light crudely reflected off cobbles and a redbrick wall.

I turned to my right. There I saw yet another spotlight, and a little beyond it there was a bentwood chair. This also had rope hanging on it, and the board that leaned against the wall was a picture of a seedy room with bare floorboards, a mattress on the floor and a window with black panes of glass in which a single bare bulb was reflected.

A feeling of nausea twisted inside my belly. I crossed the room to the closed door and pulled it open. The ceiling and the wall on my right were bare, irregular rock face, where they had taken advantage of an overhang. The lean-to wall and the floor were made of rough wooden boards. I followed this improvised tunnel in a gentle curve to the mouth of a cave. I saw there were heavy-duty, black cables on the floor and I absently noted that they must have a generator going somewhere.

I moved into the mouth of the cave. At its widest point I figured it was twenty foot across and about the same height. As I pressed forward I noticed that here too there were spotlights plugged into heavy-duty power boards.

I pushed on a little farther and saw that the cavern turned gently to the left. It became dark there, with irregular outcrops of rock and boulders. But beyond it I could see a faint glow of light and I moved on, picking my way carefully past the rocks.

As I rounded the bend the floor of the cave became sandy and flat, and the roof of the cavern opened up and rose into shadows. A cable had been hung overhead and a couple of arc lights had been suspended from it. It was empty, deserted, and a menacing, eerie feeling permeated it.

But the most bizarre thing about the place was the series of rough wooden structures that had been erected against the walls. They were cubicles, like small rooms or cells, eight foot square maybe, with four-by-four frames and plywood walls screwed in place. They had no roofs, but chicken wire had been stapled over the tops. The doors were also of ply, with heavy-duty hinges and deadbolts at top and the bottom. They all stood open, but one.

I crossed the open space, hearing my boots scraping on the sand. I paused at the bolted door, hearing my own breathing, heavy and slow. I couldn't shake the feeling of nausea, the feeling I was going to throw up at any moment. I struggled to focus my mind. What was I going to find in there? Maybe a booby-trap, a bomb, a child? Maybe all three in one.

I checked the bolts and the hinges and found no wires, so I eased the bolts back, stood aside and pulled the door open.

Nothing happened. I hunkered down and peered inside.

There was a woman. She was lying on a bare mattress. She was wearing denim shorts with frayed edges, and a torn white blouse. She had nothing on her feet, her hair was blonde and her pale face was bruised. Her lips were swollen and there was blood caked around her mouth and her nose.

I went in and hunkered down next to her. I knew who she was. I recognized her from the photographs. She was Heather, Maggie's sister. I took hold of her arm and looked at the crook of her elbow, confirming what I already knew, what I had suspected from the start. He had broken her by making her an addict.

I checked her pulse. She was alive. Left here for what? For later? For me to find? A payoff? Have her back but leave me alone? Even in my feverish state I didn't believe that.

I stood and leaned my head against the wall. They had to eat, I told myself. Maybe they didn't need to wash, but they had to eat, they had to use the john, they had to sleep and sit down some-times. There had to be more to this place. And if there was more to the place, then two got you twenty that's where Oz and his boys were.

I left Heather where she was, locked her in and made my way back through the cave and along the improvised tunnel. The first room I had come to was as it had been, but now I could see that at the far end, there was a door half-concealed behind the painting of the seedy room.

My body was aching, begging me to allow it to rest, but I ignored the pain and the exhaustion, forcing my mind to think at least two steps ahead. What would I find beyond this next door? Another improvised tunnel hugging the face of the ravine. And at the end? Living quarters, bedrooms, a kitchen, a john, a living room. It seemed to make sense.

I took a hold of the painting and pulled it away. Like the other door this one was not locked, like they were not expecting visitors.

I opened it and as I had thought I found a bare stone floor and wall. But here there was no overhang, so the outer wall had been made as a lean-to. I followed it around the face of the cliff, but did not come to another cave. Instead it led to another prefab, only this one was much bigger, and had been camouflaged under dirt, rocks and bushes. It had, like the hangar at the studio, a rolling door, which now stood open, fifteen or twenty paces away.

I squatted down, pressed against the wall, and listened, trying hard to focus my attention on the sounds coming from within the hangar. There were none. Questions kept looming in my mind, without eliciting any answers.

Why had no alarm been triggered? Were they that confident that this place would not be found? Had they not had time to install one? Why were they not swarming all over me? Why was I not dead already?

I stood and moved the remaining twenty paces with the assault rifle at my shoulder, but by the time I got to the entrance, I already knew there was nobody there.

The hangar was about the same size as the one at the studio, but using basic four-by-four pine and plywood, they had made a kitchen, a john and a few cubicles where they could sleep. I checked them out. They were more comfortable than the ones in the cave. They were at least furnished. Seven of them had double bunks with sheets, pillows and duvets. An eighth one had a double bed.

So if Oz and his boys slept here while they were filming, who slept in the cubicles in the cave?

And where was everybody now? Were they about to return?

I looked around and noticed there was no IT here. Not a single computer that I had seen. It made sense that up here on the High Ridge, among the deep ravines, there would be no signal. Even cell phones would not work up here. And that made me wonder how long they had been up here. I wondered also, how much they *didn't* know.

I went back to the little studio at the front, opened the front door and walked to the end of the tunnel. I went out on the ledge and looked west, and there, between the two massive, black hulks of the hills, I could see the broad, flat plain, and at its heart the smoldering glow of what had been the Farm.

He knew.

But if he knew, why had I not crossed them when I headed for Studio Four? Why had I not met them head on?

There could be only one reason. They had not gone to the Farm. They had seen the size of the explosion, they had seen the flames engulf the place, and they had known there was nothing to be done. All they had was either escape, or revenge. And I knew, like I knew the sun would rise tomorrow, Oz would always take revenge over escape.

I turned and ran back down the tunnel, through the small studio and back to the cave. There I slid back the bolts on the small wooden cell and yanked open the cubicle door. Heather stirred, moaned and turned over. I reached down and pulled her to her feet, feeling the agonizing tearing at my belly. I hooked her arm around my shoulders and dragged her out. Her feet stumbled. She made no effort to stand or walk. I snarled at her, "Come on! Walk! *Walk!*"

She moaned and mumbled, telling me to leave her alone. Twice she went down on her knees and I felt like a molten blade was being driven through my gut. Warm blood oozed from the bandage Maggie had bound around my waist and I felt my shirt sticking to my belly.

I dragged her up and forced her to walk, bellowing in her ear, "*Walk, dammit! Walk!*"

We entered the makeshift tunnel and the cold air made her start and open her eyes as I dragged her toward the small studio. There, as I pushed open the door she started shaking her head.

"No! No!" She said it giving it a strange, rising intonation at the end, and clawing at my chest. "He said I didn't have to! He *said* I didn't have to!"

I grabbed her shoulders and shook her. "Get a grip, Heather! We are not making movies! I am taking you home!"

Her eyes were like saucers, her pupils were black holes into a screaming void. I bundled her across the steel floor and out into the exit tunnel. She kept saying, "Where...? Where?"

"Home!" I snapped. "You're going home!"

I stepped ahead of her, gripping her emaciated arm in my left hand, and kicked open the door that gave onto the night. The desert gets cold in the dark and an icy wind blew in, making her shudder in her flimsy blouse and her shorts. I looked up at the moon. It was still smirking, cloaked in a deep turquoise mantle of smug infinity.

We started down the track of beaten earth, stumbling on loose stones and gravel. She was barefoot and every step she took made her wince and cry out in pain. I stopped and took off my boots.

"Put these on, and for crying out loud try to move a little faster."

She put on the boots and I dragged her down the path, trying to decide which pain to ignore, the one in my belly, the ones in my left foot or the ones in my right. I decided in the end to ignore them all and think about the icy cold that was making me shiver instead. I also tried to decide what Oz had done.

He'd gone first to the hotel. What had he found there? Nothing, nobody but a couple of vaguely bewildered customers. What had he done then? Oz was nothing if not unpredictable, so maybe he'd set fire to Hope. Maybe he'd burned down the hotel and killed the customers. All bets were off.

Or on.

Either way I figured what he would be really hungry for was Maggie and her parents, because they could lead him to that bastard—me—who had systematically destroyed his gang. So from the hotel he would go to Maggie's ranch. And there he would wait for her.

And for me.

With Heather dragging and scraping my boots, which were five sizes too big for her, we scraped and stumbled our way down the winding path and into the deeper darkness at the bottom of the canyon. When we finally got there, the ground leveled off and became soft sand, and she clung to me, clawing at my chest with hands like talons, looking around at the long shadows cast by the moon.

"I'm scared. Are you a friend? Does Oz know you? Are you a friend of Oz? You're not going to hurt me, right?"

I hissed at her, "Shut up!" and dragged her at a half run toward the RAM.

I found it where I had left it and snarled at Heather, "Give me my boots and get in the truck. Try not to talk."

She climbed out of my boots, looked at me like I'd hurt her feelings and she hoped I wouldn't hit her, and climbed in the cab. I pulled the boots on, swung in behind the wheel and fired up the big engine as I slammed the door. I turned the truck around and drove too fast out of the canyon and into the broad valley. Every jolt and jerk tore at the wound in my belly, sending shafts of pain through just about everywhere between my head and my feet. Out of the valley I turned left, south, and hurtled across the sand and shrubs with my headlamps on full, searching for the blacktop that would take me to Hope. At every lurch and bump Heather would scream, until I yelled at her, "*Shut up!*"

Then she clung to her seat belt and whimpered, which was only marginally better than screaming.

When we finally hit the Vazquez Road, I accelerated and settled back in the seat, trying to breathe and clear my mind.

"My name is Harry. You're Heather, Maggie's sister, right?"

She frowned at me like she wasn't sure if she was dreaming. "That was a long time ago."

"Yeah? Well now it's now. I'm taking you home to your family."

She didn't say anything, but as we approached the intersection for Hope she started to cry, covering her face with her arms. I left her to it.

All the houses were dark and the saloon was closed when we arrived. The hotel was dark too. There was no sign of life. What had I expected? I had told them to leave. I gripped the wheel and tried to think through the throbbing pain in my gut. What the hell did I do now? I had to focus and think clearly. I could not contact Maggie because Oz was still at large. I couldn't leave Heather at the hotel in case Oz showed up. I couldn't take her to the ranch, either. And if I took her to Alamogordo, Tucson or Phoenix, it would take too long and Oz would vanish again.

I had him within reach, and I had to destroy him now. Or it would be too late.

The only option I had was to call Maggie, get her to name a motel or a town not too far from Hope, and meet there. Hand Heather over and come back to finish Oz. That might work.

I pulled my cell from my pocket and dialed. It rang three times and stopped. I could hear breathing and movement in the background.

"Maggie?"

"Yes, who's this?"

"It's Harry. Is..."

"Who?"

"Harry."

"I'm sorry, I don't know any..."

There was a rustle of noise. Then another voice spoke. It was a rasp poisoned by a smile, that made the hair on your neck stand on end. I went cold inside as he spoke.

THIRTEEN

"HARRY? IS THAT YOUR NAME? HARRY? SUCH A STUPID name for a man who has caused me so much trouble. Well, you come on over, Harry. Me and the boys are going to be having a little fun with Mr. and Mrs. Jones." He laughed. It was an ugly, chilling noise. "You know the song, right?" He began to sing, "Me and Mrs., Mrs., Mrs. Jones, we got a thing, goin' on." He laughed.

"Where are you?"

"And though we know it's wrong," he went on singing, "well it's much too strong—"

"Where are you, Oz?"

"You think Mr. Jones will be jealous? I guess we'll have to wait and see."

"Where are you, asshole? You said you want me to come over. So where are you?"

"Well, at Maggie's ranch, of course. Where else, Harry? She's bein' real hospitable, too, real nice. Between you and me, I think she kind of likes me. I think we're *all* goin' to have a real cozy evening with little Maggie. You should really try and join us. We'll be waiting for you, Harry."

There was a quiet laugh and he hung up.

I was outflanked, outmaneuvered and outgunned. What had

started as a mere flesh wound was turning into a real liability, and I did not have the option to retreat. If I did not go straight to the ranch, he was going to rape and murder Hanna and Maggie, right in front of Bill's watching eyes. I had to go. I looked at Heather, sitting next to me.

"What the hell am I going to do with you?"

She seemed not to hear. She seemed calmer, almost coherent. I figured that would last till the craving started. Then she'd start getting crazy again. She said:

"Who are you?"

"That's not important. I'm going to have to take you with me." I fired up the truck. "If I leave you here you'll do something crazy, and I can't afford the time to take you somewhere safe, even if I knew where that was."

I followed the track I had driven earlier with Maggie, only in reverse. It seemed like years ago—like another life—but it was just a few hours earlier. And now four innocent people's lives were on the line. I could not afford to dwell on how things might have been different if I had done things differently. Reality was now, and now was what I had to deal with.

Eventually we came out of the desert and entered in among the fields on the 1437, which eventually became Dell City Main Street, where the road went from beaten earth to blacktop. There I pulled over onto the side of the road and killed the engine. Heather hadn't spoken all the way, but now she said, "What are you doing?"

"I hear something rattling on the rear axle."

I climbed out and hunkered down by the gas tank at the rear wheel. I pulled one of the two remaining cakes of C4 from my shirt. I broke one in half, massaged it, stuck in a detonator and pressed it up under the chassis, by the gas tank. Then I climbed back in the truck.

A couple of minutes later I turned in at the drive and as we rolled down the track I tried to predict the distribution of his men. They were fifteen all told, including Oz. Oz would be in the living room or in the kitchen. He would have four men with him, which would leave him ten men to distribute. He'd put six around the perimeter, and four upstairs, at the windows. That was what I would do in his situation.

We arrived at the gate. It was shut, but one of Oz's guys in a leather jacket and an SS officer's peaked cap came strolling up to the window. He saw Heather sitting next to me and let out a low chuckle.

"Oh man, he ain't gonna like that."

While he had been approaching the truck I had slipped the Fairbairn and Sykes out of my boot. When he'd finished talking I said, "I found the dope," and as I said it I rammed the blade of the fighting knife through his left eye and into his brain, then I levered it hard right and left.

One less.

He was too heavy to hold up and he slipped down off the blade. I reversed the truck and pulled forward again, so I was blocking the exit, and his body was concealed beneath the RAM. Then I killed the engine, climbed down and went round to get Heather. She was staring at me with wide eyes.

"What did you do?"

"Nothing. You fell asleep and dreamed. Don't think about it."

I left the Heckler and Koch and the grenades on the floor in the back, but I reached into my pants, slid my cell where no one would find it, then dumped the Sig, my knife and the C4 among the shrubs outside the gate. I pushed the gate open and somebody shouted at me.

"Hey! Where the hell d'you think you're going? Where's Mani?"

"He's checking out the truck. He said to go in."

He walked up close. His face was all gaping, angry incredulity, and for a moment I regretted leaving the knife behind. He was short and fat with a straggly, black beard. In his hand he had a mini Uzi. That weapon can fire up to nine hundred and fifty rounds per minute. That's about sixteen rounds per second. I was feverish and in pain and I knew I wasn't thinking straight, but it was clear to me that if I kicked him in the balls and I shoved that Uzi where the sun don't shine, in two seconds there'd be nothing left of him but his legs.

He gaped angrily into my face, then looked at Heather. "What the hell is she doing here?"

"Listen to me, grease ball, fifteen minutes ago I talked to your boss on the phone, and he told me to come here with her. Now, what do you want to do, go with your ugly face and demand he explain to you why he did that? Or would you rather explain to him why you're not letting us through?"

He curled his lip. "OK, wiseass. Put your hands up." He leaned back over his shoulder and shouted, "Hey, Zak! Come here, gimme a hand!"

Zak emerged from the shadows with a cigarette hanging from his mouth. He was tall and boney, and when he saw Heather he frowned. "What the fuck are you doing here?"

She sighed. "I don't have to explain shit to you, Zak."

Zak shrugged and sucked on his cigarette while Uzi frisked me. Then Uzi led us inside while Zak stood smoking, holding the smoke a little longer than you might think strictly necessary.

He led us through the kitchen, which was empty, down the short corridor and into the large living room. There was a fire burning in the hearth, the drapes were closed over the windows and Oz was sitting in a large armchair beside the fireplace. He had a beer in his hand and very black sunglasses poised on his bald head. He was at right angles to the sofa, which faced the fire; and ranged along the sofa were Maggie, beside Oz, her mother Hanna and Bill. They all looked up as we stepped in. When they saw Heather, Hanna let out a little cry and all three of them got to their feet. Maggie ran to her sister, who immediately started sobbing, and Bill and Hanna followed after, jostling each other to reach their daughter.

There were four other guys in the room, all armed and they all moved forward, shouting at Maggie and her parents to get back on the sofa. The big slob with the Uzi, who was just in front of me, put his hand on Hanna's chest and shoved her back. I was feeling too ill and too much in pain to think about what I was doing. Rage overwhelmed me and I put my whole body into a right hook into his floating ribs and his liver, and a left hook into his kidneys. He gasped and dropped to the floor, groaning and vomiting where he lay.

There was a stunned silence. I stared into Oz's eyes across the room, and a small voice in my head said, "Two down."

Oz said, "You look like shit."

To Maggie I said, "Sit down, the four of you," and as they hustled to the sofa I curled my lip at Oz. "I look a damned sight better than your Farm."

He jerked his chin at Heather. "How'd you find her?"

"I poured gasoline on Ben's balls and started playing with matches until he told me where Studio Four was."

He gave a small, wheezing laugh and shook his head. "Where have you been all my life? I think we were separated at birth, like in the Mexican soaps. You were brought up in the jungles of the Amazon by Kayapo Indians. Now you have come back to your brother."

"Yeah, something like that."

"I have a lot a questions for you."

"Is that so? Ask them while you can."

He ignored the implication and smiled. "Let's start with the least important, and save the best till last. Where are my boy Bobby, and his three pals?"

"On their way to the Gulf of Mexico."

"You killed them."

"And threw them into the Guadalupe River."

"You, on your own, with no help."

"Yeah," I said, with no expression in my voice or my face, "me, on my own, with no help. The same way I killed those pussies you sent to the studio with the sheriff."

He pointed at my belly. "You're bleeding, and you don't feel so good."

"Is that a question?"

He shook his head, slowly, smiling. "Why are you doing this?"

"I don't like assholes."

"Who do you work for, Harry? DEA? FBI? ATF?"

"God."

He threw back his head and gave a high, shrill screech of a laugh. When he looked at me again he said, "God? Seriously? *God?*"

"Yeah, he told me to clean out the trash. You look like trash, so I am cleaning you out."

"And *you* look and sound like an educated East Coast boy. I didn't know you had Flat Earthers over there. Now, answer the question, Harry, or we are going to start hurting Mrs. Jones, a lot."

"I'm an independent contractor. After the Feds screwed up the evidence at the trial, they put out feelers for an independent contractor to do the job. Word reached me and I took the contract."

He looked at his boys and gestured at me with both hands. "This," he said, "this is law and order. They raise hell because we like to ride our bikes, but look at what they do. They hire killers to murder private citizens."

I narrowed my eyes and shook my head. "You're out of your mind."

"No." He wagged a negative finger at me. "No, no, not at all. I am out of *your* mind. All the craziness is in you. To me it is all perfectly simple and clear. You, you pigs, ignoramuses, microshit humans, you see me and my boys and you go—" He put his hands to his head and released a horrific scream. Maggie, Hanna and Heather covered their ears. His boys winced and laughed nervously. "That's you," he said and did it again.

When he fell silent he stared at me with horror-struck eyes. Then he grinned, but the madness remained in his eyes.

"The fear," he said, "the madness and the fear and the disgust, they are all in you. I am a happy, hoppy bunny."

"So now you know who I am and why I am here, and you know what happened to your boys. What now?"

He put up his open hands with his thumbs joined, like he was framing a picture.

"You're a handsome man, Harry. You look like shit right now. You're *real* pale and you're sweating like a horse, but you're a handsome man. You ever been in a movie? Like the Beatles: 'They're gonna put me in the movies, they're gonna make a big star out of me!' Would you like to be in the movies, Harry?"

"You've got to be kidding."

He shook his head. "No. Tonight we are going to make a great movie. We'll call it, *The Love Sandwich: Life, Love and Death*. In which Harry the Butcher of New Mexico rapes and murders his way through the Jones family." He leered at them as they huddled together and hugged each other. Maggie looked up at me with tears in her eyes. I gave a single, small shake of my head.

He jumped suddenly to his feet, agile as a monkey. "And you know where we're going to do it? Right here, at the old studio. You will rape the women, then you will kill them all, after which I will personally guarantee your escape into Mexico, and a new identity. And you will live, for the rest of your life, with the knowledge of what you have done. I might even come and visit you from time to time, to see how you're getting on."

He gave his crazy laugh again, a horrible high-pitched scream, and did a stupid dance in front of the sofa, screaming, "*You gonna die! You gonna die! You gonna die!*"

I was feeling very weak and I knew that I would have to do something soon. I said: "I am not going to rape anybody, Oz, and the only people I am going to kill are you and your few, remaining boys."

He stopped dead and stared at me. "You ever seen a Swiss Army knife, Harry? I bet a Boy Scout like you owns one of his own. Am I right?"

I sighed and wondered about killing him right there and then.

"Harry, some of those wonderful knives have jagged-toothed saws. Have you ever seen one of those? I'll tell you what I am going to do, I am going to steadily dismember you, from your toes up, using that saw, Harry, if you do not rape these lovely ladies. And once raped, you will kill them. And all of this," he spread his arms wide, "*all* of it, your torture, the rapes, the murders, your departure to Mexico, will *all* be in the movie. It will be a work of pure *genius! I* am a genius, Harry. Truly, I have an IQ of one hundred and forty-six, and that makes me, officially, a genius. Did you know that?"

"So you'll be in this movie too."

"Only my hands, suitably clothed in black gloves. They are going to love it!"

"Who are?"

"Ha! Wouldn't you like to know?"

"Is that what you have buried at the old studio? Your list of clients?"

He stopped dead, then said, "You worked that out, huh?"

"I think you have dope and money there too, but the really important thing is your network of subscribers. They are worth a fortune to you, not just as subscribers, but also as blackmail victims."

"Well, Harry, thanks to you, tonight we will dig it all up and hightail it out of here. You will have raped and murdered this God-fearin' family, and you will have stolen the dope and the cash, and fled to Mexico, having murdered me and my brothers in the process."

I frowned, like I was interested. "So where are you going to go?"

"South." He nodded, like we were having a conversation at a cocktail party. "South to Brazil. There, with the friends and contacts I have, I can work unhindered for the rest of my life, revered as the genius I am."

He stepped away from me, then said suddenly, "See! See how

I have taken all this death and destruction you have visited upon me, and turned it," he turned his hand in the air like he was fitting a light bulb, "turned it to my benefit, like an ancient alchemist, shit into gold." His face was radiant as he looked at his boys. "Let's go make a movie."

I looked down at Uzi who was still making small, painful noises, lying in a pool of his own vomit. I stepped over to him and, with my eyes fixed on Oz's, I stamped my heel into the back of his neck. I felt the vertebrae crunch and snap. Uzi went quiet.

"OK," I said, "let's go and make your movie."

FOURTEEN

THE MOON WAS LOW BEHIND THE HOUSE, MAKING THE horizon deceptively pale. Oz gathered his men, who now numbered only twelve. With me, Maggie, Heather and their parents, that made a total of seventeen, which meant he was going to need another truck—the RAM.

He pointed at me. "You're gonna come with me in the Land Rover, with Terrier and Gob."

I interrupted. "We should go in the RAM. It's already in the drive..."

His face flushed. "I said we go in the Land Rover. Don't you fuckin'..." Then his eyes narrowed. "Check the RAM, back seat."

He was a real genius. I played along and sighed. "Fine. We go in the Land Rover. What do I care?"

A guy with thin, sandy hair and only one tooth in his mouth ran across the yard to the Dodge. He swung over the gate and pulled open the back door. After a moment he emerged holding up the assault rifle and the grenades.

"Hey, Boss! Look what I found. Sweet!"

Oz scowled at me. "You were going to try and kill me, you son of a bitch."

I narrowed my eyes at him. "Why the hell do you think I'm here, Oz? To have a meaningful dialogue with you?"

His face fell slightly and he grunted. Then he turned away and started issuing instructions again, while I contemplated the fact that I had sacrificed the assault rifle, but had, for now at least, managed to conceal the Sig, the fighting knife and the C4, on the basis that having found the one, they would not search for the other. Oz was saying:

"Mom and Dad, you go with Elmo and Jacob in the Ford. Heather and Maggie, you're with Dom and Hank. And Scotty, Knuckles, you get Rat's body from the living room, we'll bury it at the studio. You go with Teeth, Goofy and Mani, in the RAM."

He looked around, and all his boys looked at each other. Oz said, "Where's Mani?"

I didn't say anything. Oz turned and stared at me with a crazy kind of manic frown. "You killed him *too?* When? How did you *do* that? What? You're some kind of fuckin' ninja? You kill with your fuckin' *mind?*"

"Relax," he probably slipped off somewhere to smoke a joint and fell asleep."

"Yeah," he said like he wasn't sure whether to believe me or not. "Yeah," he said again and laughed. "That's probably what he did." He looked around him again. "Go find the son of a bitch! Come on! Let's find him!"

Several of them ran off, shouting his name. Oz pointed to the toothless wonder. "Mom and Dad, in the truck."

I figured he must be Elmo or Jacob, because he and a guy with too many teeth grabbed Hanna and Bill and hustled them off to a Ford pickup.

"Dom, Hank, take the bitches! Come on! Where's Mani?"

Dom and Hank grabbed Maggie and Heather and dragged them off to another truck, while Scotty, Knuckles, Teeth and Goofy came back shrugging and spreading their hands.

"We can't find him nowhere, Oz."

Oz gave me a long stare. If stares could disembowel people

and eat their hearts, I would have been a hollow cavity right then. As it was, I studied his face and wondered how many hours he had left to live. Maybe he saw that in my eyes because he looked away. "OK, everybody aboard, let's go make this fuckin' movie!"

The four merry monsters shuffled off toward the RAM but I didn't move. I jerked my chin toward the Gulf of Mexico and said, "It's going to rain."

"So what?"

"That plain is going to flood."

"Yeah? Don't worry about it. We won't be there that long. Come on, quit stalling. Terrier, Gob, you get in the back. This asshole does anything, cut his throat."

That made them whoop a couple of times. They liked the idea. That was proof their boss was a genius. As they climbed in the back I reached in my jeans and scratched my ass. It wasn't an action these guys were likely to notice as anything out of the ordinary. When I withdrew my hand I slipped my cell into my jacket pocket.

Scotty backed up the Dodge and turned it around, while Goofy pulled open the gate. Elmo, the toothless wonder pulled up behind him with Bill and Hanna, and Dom, with Maggie and Heather, positioned himself next while we waited to follow at the rear. I said:

"I need to piss."

Oz looked at me like I'd said I was from Mars. "*What?*"

"I need to urinate, Oz. It happens, you drink, your bladder fills up and then you need to piss! Is that a problem?"

"Jesus Christ!"

"You want me to piss in the truck?"

"No!"

"Right! I didn't think so. So I'll go by the damned gate where you can watch me."

I climbed out and slammed the door, then walked over to where I had dropped the Sig, the knife and the C4. My hands were shaking and my breathing was ragged, and the pain from the wound was a deep, constant throb. I was exhausted from trying to ignore it.

I leaned against the fence and made like I was peeing. After a moment I swore, like I'd stained my boot. I scraped it on the ground. Somebody honked. I hunkered down and grabbed a handful of sand to rub on the toe. Oz leaned out of his window.

"Come on! What the hell are you doing?"

"I peed on my boot! Get off my back, Oz!"

"Come on, already!"

I stood and returned to the cab, slamming the door as I settled into my seat. Oz honked and the RAM pulled away. We followed in convoy. We went at a steady pace, moving south through Dell City, which lay dark and sleeping, spread out around us, and then east along William Street, in a long, unwavering line through the fields, toward the broad, endless sands and death.

It didn't take long. The road was perfectly straight and it was less than ten miles to the old studio. Pretty soon we had left the fields behind us and we were out in the White Sands Flats. The moon had gone. She was done mocking me. The sky had darkened and the Milky Way was a luminous path across heaven.

Eventually I recognized the dark shape of the studio building looming ahead on the right. I shuddered and slipped my hands in my pocket and pressed lock and the volume button at the same time.

It was a shock, even for me, though I was expecting it. There was a massive flash of light. A fraction of a second later the air slammed into us like a steel wall. We were driving on dirt, so there was no squeal of brakes like you get on blacktop. We skidded and swerved and next thing there was another explosion and a huge fireball leapt curling up into the night sky.

It was a fraction of a second and suddenly the trucks were piling into each other. I smashed my right elbow into Oz's chin and swung down from the cab before he'd stopped the truck. It collided with the rear of Dom's truck as I wrenched open the rear door and plunged the Fairbairn and Sykes into the side of Terrier's neck. I left it there while I pulled his Taurus revolver from his pants and put two rounds into Gob's head. Then I retrieved my knife and ran to Dom's truck. Maggie had already climbed out and was pulling Heather out. I grabbed her and made her look at me.

"Maggie! *Maggie!*"

"What?"

"Look at me! Listen to me! Go to the house. Take your parents and Heather. Stay there." She nodded. "Go! Now!"

Dom was unconscious behind the wheel but Hank was standing, covering his face with his hands on the far side of the truck, saying, "Oh God, oh God..."

I ran to Elmo and Jacob's truck and wrenched open the back. The heat from the burning wreckage at the front was intense. Bill was already climbing out the far side and was cowering away from the flames, making his way around to get his wife. I took hold of Hanna and pulled her out. Maggie was beside me, dragging Heather with her by her hand. I handed her mother over.

"The fire might spread. There could be more explosions. Get them out of here!"

They ran staggering toward the studio and I peered in the driver's window. Elmo looked at me with blood all over his face and his toothless mouth gaping. The windscreen was shattered and half of it was in his face. He opened the door and fell out. On the far side Jacob was slumped, bleeding profusely from his face. I pulled the Sig from my waistband and shot him in the head. Elmo was getting to his knees, but he never made it. I put a slug in the back of his neck and the pain stopped. For him, at least.

"Drop it."

I turned. It was Oz. He had a Smith and Wesson 29 pointed at my head. It was steady. It wasn't shaking. His eyes were crazy. Behind him he had Dom, who looked very sick, and Hank who was bleeding from a cut on his forehead. They both had guns, though I doubted right then they'd know what to do with them.

"You don't know," said Oz. "You just don't know."

I dropped the Sig in the dirt. "What don't I know, Oz?"

"You don't know how deeply I hate you. How badly I want to hurt you."

"OK, but whatever you do to me, you should do it at the studio, because these trucks could explode at any minute."

"Move."

We walked around the twisted, burning Dodge. Inside you could see the ghastly carbonizing figures engulfed in fire. As we passed them a voice in my head told me, "Two left. And then Oz.."

The wind had dropped, but there was an icy breeze coming in from the south. Ahead I could see Maggie and her family heading for the house, but Oz roared at them. "*You! I told you we're going to make a fucking movie! Go to the fucking studio!*" They stopped and hesitated. He screamed at them, "*Move!*"

They joined us and we were herded across the yard toward the big hulk of the hangar. As we neared it he slammed the butt of the revolver into my back and screamed a high shrill scream, then pounded again, punctuating his words, "*Open-the-fucking-door!*"

The pain was crippling, piercing my chest and sending my lungs into spasm. I gripped the door, used it for support and heaved, rolling it back. He was down to two, semi-incapacitated men, but I knew right then that Oz had never been more dangerous than he was now. And I had never been weaker.

He pointed into the corner and snapped at Dom, "Light."

Dom walked unsteadily into the shadows. I heard the loud "clack!" of a metal latch, and after a moment the whole hangar was flooded with dead, sterile light.

"OK." Oz waved the big cannon toward the far end of the hangar, where Maggie and I had seen the sofa. It sat there now, like a mad nightmare, floodlit, a motionless, unreal stage set waiting for a horrific, real act of extreme violence.

We moved, strange and stiff across the vast floor until we stopped in front of the set. Two spotlights bathed the sofa in light. The sofa sat and waited. Oz snapped, "Camera! Where's the camera? And the mic! I want this son of a bitch to have sound!" He thrust his face into mine. "I want to hear *every damned scream and every time they fuckin' beg for pity!*"

Hank went away and came back after a couple of minutes with a tripod and a small video camera, while Dom brought a boom with a mic. While they were setting it up, Oz pointed at Hanna.

"You, get on the sofa."

Bill stepped in front of her. "No," he said, "you son of a bitch. You are not gonna do this to my wife."

Maggie gripped his arm and stood shoulder to shoulder with him. I said, "Bill, don't—"

But Oz stepped up to him and pointed a finger in his face. "I oughta kill you, old man. But I'm not going to. You know why? Because after he—," he pointed at me, "after he rapes her and your daughters, *he* is gonna kill you. Now you have a choice, old man. Either you get out of my way now or I start removing pretty little Maggie's fingers one by one!"

Hanna screamed and started clawing at her daughter, pushing her husband out of the way. "*No! No! No, Maggie, no, I will do it. I will do it. Don't hurt my babies! Please!*"

Oz laughed suddenly and leered at me. "I think she likes you, tiger!"

Bill's face had flushed crimson and I knew he was about to do something stupid. I took a long step and delivered a straight lead to the tip of his jaw. His eyes rolled in his head and he went gently down in his wife and his daughters' arms.

Oz scowled into my eyes. "I wanted him to watch."

I held his eye. "To watch, he needs to be alive. If he kept going he was going to get himself killed."

"Camera's ready, Boss."

"So's the mic. We ready to roll."

He glanced at his two remaining boys and turned to Hanna, who was hunkered down on the floor with her daughters, stroking Bill's face.

"You, on the sofa."

She looked at me with pleading in her eyes. I made a microscopic shake of the head.

"We'd better do as he says, Hanna." She stood and went to the sofa, hugging herself, and sat. Her face crumpled and she began to weep.

I said to Oz, "I can't do this."

There was nothing but sneering contempt in his face. "What are you talking about?"

"I have my belly cut open, I am losing blood, I can't remember when I last slept, and these are my friends! How the hell do you expect me to rape them?"

He slapped me, hard, open hand. The fire welled in my stomach and I had to fight to hold it down. "Think of it this way, Boy Scout, if you don't rape her, I will. And I am *really* gonna hurt her. So do what you need to do, then get over there and *rape her!*"

He looked past me at Maggie and Heather. "And you two, wake up the old man. I want him to see this." He laughed. "This is gonna be good."

I knew I could not take him, and Dom and Hank in the state I was in. Dom and Hank were still shaken from the explosion, I might just manage them. But Oz was built like an ox, he was fresh and he was armed with a weapon I knew he would not hesitate to use. A weapon that does not wound. You take a .44 Magnum slug in your arm, you will lose that arm, you take it in the leg and you will probably lose the leg. Out here, that would mean death.

I looked at Hanna sobbing on the sofa. I looked at Heather, and Maggie, cradling her father's head in her lap. He had his face covered with his hands and he was sobbing too. Maggie looked up at me. I said, "I am sorry."

FIFTEEN

I UNDID MY BELT BUCKLE AND SPOKE AS I REMOVED MY belt.

"Where is it buried?"

"What?"

"You heard me, Oz. Don't keep asking me, 'What?' Where is the stuff buried?"

"What is this now? We're about to shoot a damn snuff movie and he asks me, 'Where is it buried?' Would you please go and rape that woman, and kill her?"

I heard Hanna gasp and let out a small cry.

"Will you shut up and listen to me, Oz? I thought you were supposed to have a massive IQ. So use it. Think. I am physically exhausted. I am burned out. So I am not in a physical condition to...," I shrugged, "...you know."

He cackled. "You got LDS, limp dick syndrome!" He cackled again, looking at Dom and Hank, who laughed too, though with less feeling. I ignored him and went on.

"So, I'm thinking that what could motivate me, and make things work, is a snort of coke and a share of the cash." His face froze, but you could see his brain working behind his eyes. "And," I added, "you could film the snorting before the act."

He grinned. "You know, for once, you had a good idea. That's not bad. I like that." His smile faded and his eyes took on a diamond hard glint. "What do you mean, a share of the cash?"

I shrugged. "I figured as there are only three of you left, you were going to share it sixty-forty. Sixty for you and twenty each for these bozos." He gave a noncommittal grunt. I gestured at Hank. "So kill him and give me his share. Then you can send me to Mexico with some money in my pocket. Otherwise I'm going to be trying to do what you're asking me to do, but I'll be worried sick about what's going to happen to me when I get to Mexico."

Throughout the speech, Hank was staring at Oz with a slack jaw and dull, frightened eyes. "You ain't gonna kill me, is ya, Boss?"

"Of course not. Don't be stupid."

I ignored them both and asked, "I mean, what kind of money are we talking about? If this movie is popular with your client list, is there any reason why we can't make more?" I laughed, looking him in the eye. "It would be like the *Emmanuelle* movies back in the '70s. *Harry, Harry in Mexico, Harry in the Philippines, The Awakening of Harry*!"

He had started to laugh too. We were like two crazy men, staring into each other's faces, laughing, shouting at each other. He was saying, "And you are like this crazy killer, just going all over the fuckin' world, killing bitches everywhere you go, man! That's awesome."

I nodded. "So where is it buried?"

His laughter died and his eyes swiveled side to side. "I don't know. How do I know I can trust you?"

I shouted at him. "*Of course you can't trust me! But look at me, for crying out loud! I'm fighting for my life here! You have all the aces! You think I'm in any condition to cause trouble?*" I paused and pointed at the Smith and Wesson in his hand and spoke more quietly. "You want a guarantee? There's your guarantee. I am spent, burned out. Give me a snort and enough cash to survive in Mexico, and you win."

He shoved his chin toward Hanna. "What about them?"

"Tie them up. They're not going anywhere."

He looked at Hank and Dom and nodded. Hank hesitated and repeated, "You really ain't gonna kill me, are you, Boss?"

"Come on, Hank! You're my boy! 'Course I'm not gonna kill you! There's plenty to go around. Don't you worry."

Hank smiled and followed Dom to the film set where, one by one, they tied up the women and Bill. I knew Maggie and her father were staring at me with hatred and reproach in their eyes. I couldn't face them, so I turned my back and put my belt back on, but I didn't slip it through the loops. I left it hanging loose.

When Dom and Hank were done, Oz sent them to get shovels. He was looking at me sidelong and getting nervous. I said, "Are we going to do this or are you going to lose your nerve and freak out on me?"

He didn't answer. He just stared at me along his eyes.

Hank and Dom came back and we followed them out into the yard. Then they hung back, looking at Oz to lead the way. He went to the corner of the hangar and counted out ten paces to a dilapidated wooden fence. He clambered over it and counted out sixty paces more. Then he turned sharp right and counted another fifteen paces. We were in the middle of a featureless plain of white sand, dotted with shrubs. And now I could see what I had not been able to see before: the long, broad flattened shape of a landing strip.

The wind was picking up, becoming blustery, and on the horizon the clouds were building into huge thunderheads.

Oz grinned at me. "If you did not know the exact number of steps, and where to take them, you could search this place for a hundred years and not find it." He took a step closer, peering into my face. "I been waiting for the opportunity to come and get this stuff, but I was sure the Feds were watching me. Seems like after you arrived they stopped."

"I told you, I was paid to kill you. They could not be witness to that."

He gurgled a laugh. "Yeah, I guess not. Bet they'd like to be, though." He pointed down at where he was standing. "Dig here, boys. It's about three foot down."

He stepped aside and Hank and Dom started digging. I said, "What's in there?"

He grinned and stroked the exquisite revolver in his hand.

"Do you know how many people I have killed?"

"Is that supposed to be an answer?"

He looked at me and his eyes were beyond cold. They were amused at his own lack of feeling, at his own evil.

"*I* don't know. I have lost count. I—do not recall—all the people I have killed. Can you believe that?"

I shrugged. "Sure. You're an evil son of a bitch, Oz. I don't think there is anything you could tell me that would surprise me."

The amusement faded from his eyes. He jerked his chin at me.

"You think you're the good guy, come to punish the bad guy. You're the avenging angel and I am the devil—good come to punish evil. But you don't understand the half of it, Harry. Good does not punish evil. But let me tell you something, Evil is its own justitioner. Evil is its own nemesis. You are not the instrument of God. You are the instrument of evil, whereby evil punishes itself."

I felt the ice cold of the desert seep through me. I didn't say anything, and after a moment Hank said, "We found it, Boss. It's here."

Oz stepped over and I opened my belt. I stepped up behind Hank and slipped it over his head and around his neck. I squeezed hard, twisted and turned my back on him, leaning forward, pulling hard, like I was carrying a heavy sack. I heard him choking, felt his legs jerk wildly, and pulled tighter until he went into a wild spasm. Finally he sagged and went still. Then I dropped him to the ground.

Oz and Dom were standing motionless, staring at me. They were very serious. Dom said, "You didn't have to do that."

I nodded at the hole and asked Oz again, "What's in there?"

"Ten Ks of coke, twenty Ks of heroin and two million bucks in cash."

"Is that all?"

"Yeah."

"You're lying."

"Fuck you."

"You have a list of your clients in there. What is it, a little black book?" I watched his face and knew I was almost right. He said, "So what? What's it to you?" To Dom he said, "Go get the Land Rover. Bring it here. We'll load the stuff in, make the movie and get the hell out of here before the storm breaks. Suddenly I'm sick of this place."

Dom turned and crossed the plain toward the road at a half run. I said, "So what now?"

He chuckled. "What now?"

"Let them go, Oz. They're nothing to you. They probably won't even go to the cops. And if they do you'll be long gone."

He shook his head. "You know, sometimes you really impress me. I mean, seriously. What you did just there with Hank. You know, *right on!* You are one motherfuckin' evil son of a bitch. But then you come out with this chicken-shit stuff, like, let 'em go." He made a mocking, weeping face. "Poor things, let 'em go, Oz, be nice." He spat. "Bullshit. First you rape them, then you kill them. That's what I do. It's who I am."

I nodded. "OK."

"OK? That's it? OK?"

I shrugged. "What else can I say? You hold all the cards, and the cannon."

The sound of the powerful Land Rover engine came to us across the predawn dark. It whined and growled across the shrubs and potholes behind the dual glare of the headlamps. When it came level with us it turned east and backed up so the trunk was almost level with the hole. He killed the engine and the lights and jumped down from the cab. Oz said, "We load the money, we leave the dope here."

He jumped in the hole, grabbed a plastic pack of coke and tossed it to me.

"We take one, for the sake of art!"

He cackled and passed two sports bags up to Dom, who slung them in the back of the Land Rover. Then I saw him grab a medium-sized ledger, about twelve inches long, and slip it under his jacket.

On an impulse I said, "Is Judge Casper Williams in that book?"

He stopped dead and stared at me. "You got a big mouth, Harry. Keep pushing me and we won't make no movie. I'll just shoot the whole damned lot of you."

They pushed Hank into the hole and shoveled the sand back over the dope and the body. We clambered in the truck and rolled and jolted back to the studio, where he drove right into the hangar. Dom jumped out and pulled the door closed and Oz drove the truck right up to the set. There we climbed out and Oz stood looking down at Maggie and Heather.

"Dawn'll be here in about an hour. Once the good, God-fearing folk of Dell City see that column of black smoke trailing up from that truck out there, they will call the sheriff and he will come and investigate. By that time, we need to be long gone." He turned to me. "So we cannot wait no longer. You snort your coke, you do your job and we go."

"What about the money?"

"You'll get your money. Delay another minute and I'll blow your fuckin' brains out and do the job myself."

I leaned in the Land Rover and took the pack of coke off the back seat. Dom was setting up the microphone. I stood beside him while Oz set up the camera and put the package on the hood of the truck. I did it like it was the most natural thing in the world. I put my boot on the bumper and drew my knife from my boot. Then I stepped behind Dom, placed my left hand over his mouth, pinching his nose, and drove the blade through his neck.

Oz turned, hearing Dom slump to the ground. I sprang at

him as he reached for his weapon. His neck was swollen and his face was crimson. He was screaming, "*You fucking son of a bitch! I'll kill you! I'll fucking destroy you!*"

In my condition I was too slow, and he was fast. He pistol-whipped my face, gashing my cheek, then pounded me in the belly with his right fist, rupturing the last remaining stitches. The pain was indescribable and for a second I blacked out as I hit the ground.

When I regained consciousness he was not coming after me. He was advancing on Maggie, pointing the gun at her and looking back at me. The veins were bulging in his head and spittle was flying from his lips as he screamed.

"*I'll make you suffer! I'll make you suffer every day for the rest of your life! I'll kill everyone you care for. I will cut your fucking tendons! I will make you suffer!*"

I grabbed the knife from where it had fallen. I could taste the blood in my mouth, and I could feel the warm ooze from my gaping wound. It was more stimulating than coke could ever be. I roared and charged him. He didn't know whether to shoot Maggie or turn the gun on me. He had one second to decide, and he took too long.

As he brought the revolver around I slashed at his wrist. I missed, but I cut deep into forearm. He screamed and dropped the revolver. I slashed at him backhanded, but he staggered away. I went after him with my last shred of strength. Blood was gushing from his arm and he was gripping at it with his left hand. I grabbed his jacket and wrenched him toward me. He writhed and twisted and the jacket came away in my hand. He turned and ran. I staggered back, bent to pick up the Smith and Wesson, and let off one shot as he bolted through the door.

I took a couple of steps and saw his jacket lying at my feet, with the medium-sized ledger protruding from the pocket.

I picked it up and slung it in the back of the Land Rover, then I went and cut Maggie's bonds. I gave her the knife and leaned against the side of the truck, trying to cling on to consciousness.

A moment later she was standing in front of me, cupping my face in her hands.

"Are you all right? Are you OK?"

"What the hell were you doing at the ranch, Maggie? I told you to take your family to Phoenix."

"I had to get things from home, when we got there he was waiting."

The room moved, tilted. I blinked a couple of times, trying to bring her into focus. "Next time, just do what I say, will you? You have to drive," I added. "I can't. We have to get out of here, fast. Go via Hope. Once they see the smoke from the trucks, there will be people coming from Dell City. Maybe the sheriff."

Bill opened the big door while Maggie turned the Land Rover around. I killed the lights and clambered in the front passenger seat, Bill got in the back with his wife and Heather, and we moved out of the hangar and onto the road to Hope.

As we accelerated down the long, straight track toward the Guadalupe River, the horizon was turning gray and the sky above was oppressive with heavy, gunmetal clouds. I had my window open, letting the cool dawn air batter my face. I tried to lose consciousness, but the pain was too intense and kept drawing me back. Over the mountains, the first clap of thunder rolled across the inky sky.

Maggie spoke, half to herself. "She's comin'..." I looked at her. She was driving without lights so we wouldn't be seen, leaning forward, hunched over the steering wheel.

"What happens now?" she said, suddenly. "He gets away? Everything he's done goes unpunished? He escapes to Mexico and does it all over again?"

"He's not going to Mexico," I said with half a voice.

"What? He said he was going to Mexico."

"He is not going to Mexico. He is going to come back to the ranch, or to the hotel."

"What are you talking about, Harry? Why?"

"Because I have two million dollars he believes are his. But more than that, because I have his ledger, and this ledger has details of all the people who have been his clients, or have conspired and cooperated with him to create his ring. It's in his jacket, and when I hand it over to the Feds, it will be enough to put a lot of people in prison for a very long time."

She was quiet for a while, rattling fast along the dark road. Above, thunder rumbled again. Finally she spat the words, "Prison is too good for that bastard!"

I shook my head. "He's not going to prison, Maggie."

She swung round to look at me like I was crazy. "What? Why? This is new evidence! They must be able to charge him with a new crime! Conspiracy to..."

I cut across her. "He's not going to prison, because I am going to kill him."

We did the rest of the journey in silence. Eventually, as dawn broke behind the heavy ceiling of cloud, we pulled in to Maggie's farm. I climbed carefully down from the Land Rover and Maggie and Hanna helped me into the kitchen, while Bill took the truck round back and hid it in one of the barns.

I sat, and Hanna hurried away to get towels, bandages and dressing, while Maggie put a saucepan of water on to heat, then went to help her mother. Heather sat opposite me at the big, wooden table. I studied her face. She was pale and drawn, and had a fine line of perspiration on her lip.

"You're a doctor," I said. "I need a doctor."

She shook her head. "I can't. You should have brought some stuff back with you."

"You're going cold turkey?"

She nodded. "Yes."

SIXTEEN

SHE PULLED HER CHAIR AROUND AND SAT CLOSE BESIDE me, looking hard into my face and speaking fast, in a hushed voice.

"I don't know what you think of me, who or what you think I am, or what you believe has happened here, but I have to tell you, Harry, I am not an addictive personality. Oz took me and physically forced me to become an addict. I am *physically, chemically* addicted to heroin. But I am not an addict. I am not a *junkie!*"

She spat the word out, like it made her sick. I tried to think through the pain, to what she was trying to tell me and why it was important.

"I'm not here to judge anybody, Heather. I just want one thing—"

"Oz."

I nodded. "Yeah, Oz."

"I want to help you. I hate that bastard more than you can imagine, but I haven't got long. Pretty soon I am going to be craving so bad I would kill my own mother to get a fix. Until that happens, I can help you, but only if you can get me one last fix."

I shook my head. "I can't get you a fix, Heather. I can barely stand on my feet."

She closed her eyes. "I know that, but did you bring anything with you? I saw you had a packet back there. Is there anything in the truck?"

"The packet was coke and I left it back at the studio. The heroin is all where he buried it, in the field."

"You didn't bring anything?"

"No."

"If we could just get a hold of some, a few grams, Harry, I could help you."

Her eyes were becoming wild and she was sweating on her brow and on her lip.

I shook my head. "Forget it, Heather. I didn't bring anything, and there is no way of getting it. The place will be crawling with sheriff's deputies and firemen by now. You need to lock yourself in a room and get through this."

"Jesus!" She rubbed her face with her palms. A moment later her mother and sister came in. Maggie stopped and stared at her a moment. "Heather?"

Heather shook her head. "I can't. You'll have to do it."

"Heather, for Christ's sake…"

"I *can't!*" She held out her hands. They were trembling badly. There was a moment of awkward silence. The truth was an unwelcome intruder. The door opened and Bill came in, saw the scene and froze. Heather blurted out, "I'm an addict! OK? You can't trust me and you can't rely on me. I may as well be fucking dead! The best thing you can do is lock me in a room upstairs and forget me!" She became shrill. "It's what everyone has done for the last months. A few more fucking hours shouldn't make any difference!"

Hanna suddenly seemed to come alive. She rushed across the kitchen, negotiating the big table, and threw her arms around her daughter, stroking her hair and whispering, "Baby, baby," to her.

I spoke to Maggie, who was watching her sister with distressed eyes. I said, "We're running out of time. We need to lock Heather in a room where she can't hurt herself." I turned my head to

Hanna and Heather. "But I need to know, what will Oz do now? He's badly hurt. Where will he go?"

Heather stared at me like I had asked her what color her panties were. "What?"

I closed my eyes a second, fought down the pain and the growing impatience. "Oz is going to come back here. He is going to kill all of you. Then he is going to try to kill me. Right now, the one thing standing between you and your family, and death, is me. But time is running out, so try to focus, Heather. Where will Oz go to fix the cut in his arm? Has he got friends, allies? If so, where? Were the guys that were with him the whole gang, or are there more followers?"

She stared around the kitchen like she was searching for the answers to my questions. "There's a clinic in Dell City. He'll go there to get his arm fixed. Then I guess he'll go to Phoenix."

Maggie started unbuttoning my shirt. I said, "Why Phoenix?"

"He has friends there."

I winced with pain as Maggie started removing the sticking plaster and the dressing. A wave of nausea washed through me as she pulled it away. My skin went cold and I felt the sweat break out on my brow. Maggie stared at the wound and said, "Sweet Jesus!"

"Great bedside manner, Doc. Bill, take Heather upstairs, choose a room and lock her in. Take out anything she could use to hurt herself. The next hours are going to be tough."

He put his arm around her and guided her toward the door. Her eyes were wide with terror. I bit back the pain as Maggie started washing the wound and said, "Heather."

She turned back to look at me. "You're the only one who knows how to do this. If you can guide us, advise us..."

She shook her head and started sobbing. I gave Bill the nod and closed my eyes again, trying to focus on something that wasn't the pain; trying to think about how long we had, and what steps I had to take.

Maggie said, "OK, this is going to hurt."

"Thanks."

She was quick and thorough, using hot water, soap and a cloth. It was one of the most painful things I have ever experienced, and when she was done, without warning, she doused the wound with surgical spirit. Blasphemy was the best thing that came out of my mouth right then. I think Hanna gasped, but I didn't really give a damn.

I had bellowed enough sacrilege to turn an atheist's hair gray and make a Satanist drop to his knees and pray for forgiveness, when Maggie started saying "OK, OK, OK," over and over, and spreading a soothing white cream over the wound. She laid gauze over it and taped it down.

"What about the stitches?" I said.

She handed me a couple of painkillers and I knocked them back with a glass of water. She said, "A couple have ripped the skin. The others have held. You have got to go to a doctor."

"Not yet."

"If that gets infected you could die."

I looked her in the eye. "Maggie, you listen to me. Your mother, your father and your sister *will* die. No 'ifs.' He *will* come back. And he won't come back looking just for me. He will come back looking for all of us. This guy is seriously crazy. He wants revenge, and he has it in his head that the best way he can hurt me, is to hurt you."

"I know that, Harry! You think I don't know that? But we *have* to get you to a..."

"You have to leave."

She stopped dead and I saw Hanna slowly put her hands to her mouth. Maggie shook her head. "No."

"Listen to me, I have been doing this since I was eighteen years old. I am done. I'm done with fighting and done with killing. If the last thing I do is take down Oz, then my life will have been worthwhile. But if you, and Hanna and Bill, and Heather, if you all go down too, all this will have been for nothing. Get your family to safety, and I will take care of Oz."

Her face began to crumple, her bottom lip went in under her even, white teeth. "I'll come back. I'll take them to Alamogordo. I'll contact the Alamogordo Police Department and come back to get you!"

I smiled with more swank than I felt. "And sentence me to the next twenty years in a state penitentiary?" I laughed. "I'll call you when it's over. Take the money in the Land Rover, get your sister cleaned up. Leave the Land Rover out front, use your dad's car. Get out of here. I'll call you tomorrow."

The door opened and Bill came in. Hanna went to him and spoke softly. He stared at me with infinite sadness and then went out into the gray dawn. Maggie came and reached for my hand.

"I want to see you again."

I nodded. "I want you to write down a name and a number, in New York." I gave it to her and she shook her head. "Who is this?"

"Don't throw that money away. Get this guy to invest it for you."

Her eyes went wide and her cheeks flushed with anger. "*Harry!*"

"Listen to me, Maggie. This guy will look after you. You tell him..."

She huffed and scowled at me. "Like I give a damn!"

"You tell him," I insisted more quietly, "that Harry Bauer sent you."

The anger drained from her face and she held my eye a moment. "Harry Bauer."

"That's between you and me."

"She smiled. "How d'you do, Harry Bauer?"

"Usually, I do a damned sight better than this." I held out my hand and we shook, gently. "How d'you do, Maggie Jones?" She leaned down and gave me a kiss.

I said, "Now go and take care of your family. And this time, Maggie, do it."

She sighed and left the room to go and get Heather. I sat for a couple of minutes focusing on my breathing until Bill rolled around in the Land Rover. Then I got to my feet and went out into the heavy, sultry morning. The wind had risen slightly, and you could feel the static in the air. Over in the east, over the mountains, flashes of sporadic light illuminated the horizon.

Bill climbed down from the cab. I limped over to him. His voice sounded hollow in the leaden stillness.

"You should come with us. Ain't no sense dyin' at the hands of that bastard. You got enough evidence to put him away for life."

I smiled and nodded. "That bastard ran a child pornography ring, Bill, made a lot of money from it, and he and the guys who ran it got off scot-free." I paused, looking him in the eye. "You know what they'd call Oz in a state penitentiary?"

He frowned and shrugged. "Don't know as I care."

I said, "Sir, they'd call him sir. That bastard is going to die in the next twenty-four hours, or I am going to die trying."

"Fair enough, Harry. I can respect that."

He gave me the keys to the truck and I watched him go back to get his own car. When he was out of sight I walked to the gate. Mani was lying there in the dust, his arms and legs broken where the truck had rolled over him. I ducked under the fence and found the one and a half pounds of C4 in the weeds, then I fished through Mani's clothes till I found his cell and his Glock. It wasn't my favorite weapon, but it would do. Then I made my way back toward the house.

When I got back to the kitchen, Bill was pulling around in his Chevy, and Maggie and Hanna were emerging from the house with Heather held between them. They put her in the back seat of the car and Maggie came to me and placed her hands on my chest.

"Come with us."

The stillness in the air was menacing. I shook my head. "I can't."

She closed her eyes and I could see her fighting back the tears. "Please be careful."

"That I can promise. I'll call you. Go, every minute counts."

She kissed me again, then ran to the car. A moment later, after the door had slammed with a dull echo, I saw it roll away. There was no trailing cloud of dust now, in that leaden, humid air. No birds sang, nothing moved. There was only a nameless, impending menace.

I went back inside and with what little strength I had left I made myself a protein bomb of three eggs, a half pound of bacon and four breakfast sausages. I washed this down with a pot of strong, black coffee and sat at the kitchen table for a while with my eyes closed, unable to move.

Finally I got the medium-sized ledger and laid it on the table, and with a second pot of coffee, I set about reading through it. It was an education. He had listed every person who had ever subscribed to his network, how much they had paid, on what dates, what they had signed up for and what "extra products and services" they had bought. Some, perhaps the majority, had signed up for online movies only; others, a select but sizeable group, had paid substantial sums for the privilege of joining a deeper network of child prostitution. Every detail had been recorded, and every detail could be followed up and traced by forensic accountants and investigators. Oz had every single one of them over a barrel.

At a rough guess I calculated there must be about two thousand names, and for some reason that number meant something to me. I realized why when at the back I found an appendix of names and their relationship to Oz and his organization beside it.

Most of the names I had never heard of, but near the top, listed as co-founder, was Abdul ben Elahi. That was the name I had tried to remember when the brigadier first briefed me on Oz. A handful of the other names would make the national news, and went a long way to explaining why he had avoided arrest and conviction for so long, in spite of the monstrous nature of his crimes.

I photographed every page and sent it to the brigadier. Then I took Mani's phone and photographed the cover. I found Oz in his address book and sent him the picture with the message, "You went in such a hurry, you left this behind, and two million bucks. I'll be waiting when you come to collect them."

I was surprised at how soon he replied. The cell rang. I answered.

"Yeah."

"You cut me real bad. I had to see a doctor."

For a moment my brain ached. I shook my head and closed my eyes. "I don't know how to even begin to answer that, Oz. I don't care."

"You're a son of a bitch. I'm going to kill you."

"Yeah, yeah, yadda, yadda. You want the ledger and your money?"

"Of course I do." He paused, then, "You want to finish this, you and me? Where are you?"

"At the ranch where we met last night."

"Are you alone?" There was a sneer in his voice.

"Are you?"

"You fuckin' know I am. You killed all my boys, you mother-fucker! I'm gonna eat your fuckin' heart!"

"Sure, whatever. Yeah, I'm alone."

"You ain't got your army of girls and old men to help you?"

"They're gone and you won't find them. Your beef is with me."

He grunted something like a chuckle. "OK, I need breakfast and I need some sleep, and I need to get some gas. Gimme a couple of hours."

Something in his voice, something I could not identify, crawled through my skin.

"Oz, if I see anyone other than you arrive at this ranch, I will pour gasoline all over this ledger, and your two million bucks, and your coke and your heroin, and I will set fire to it all. You understand that I will do that, right?"

He was quiet for a long while, then he said, "Yeah, I understand that you will do that, yeah. But you know what, asshole? I only got a cut on my arm, and I enjoy pain. You got your belly cut open, you're burned out, and you *don't* enjoy pain. So I don't *need* nobody to ride with me. I am going to drive down there, I am going to beat you to a pulp, and then I am going to gut you and hang you from your own fuckin' intestines. Now let me ask you, you do understand that I will do that, right?"

"No," I said quietly. "I don't understand that, Oz, but I do look forward to seeing you very soon."

And I hung up.

I had no idea how he would come. He could come from any direction, in a truck or a car, on a bike or on foot. He was unpredictable. He might brazen it out and come rolling down the track, or he might wait till dark and come across the fields. He knew I'd wait for him, because he knew all I really cared about was finishing him. Outside a clap of thunder sounded overhead and rolled across the sky.

I made a small tour of the house. It was like late evening. Barely any light filtered through the windows. There was not much I could do to prepare, besides place the ledger where he could not retrieve it. Then I locked all the doors and the windows, and went upstairs. I chose the bedroom at the northeastern corner of the house and lay down. What I desperately needed before he arrived was sleep.

SEVENTEEN

THE RINGING OF MY CELL JARRED ME OUT OF A DARK nightmare. I looked at the screen and saw it was Maggie.

"Yeah, what?"

"Harry, I don't know what to do!"

My brain struggled. Needles of pain pierced my belly as I tried to sit up.

"What are you talking about? Do about what?"

Through the window I could see huge, lowering clouds boiling. The air was muggy and electric. I looked at the clock. It was just ten AM. I felt a sudden sinking nausea in my gut as I remembered someone was coming to kill me. Maggie was babbling.

"Mom needed to go to the john, we decided to have coffee. She went to the can. We were just having a quick cup of coffee, God *damn* it!"

"Maggie, slow down and be clear. What has happened? Be precise."

"She's *gone!*"

"Your mother has gone?"

"*No! Not my mom! Heather!*"

I swore violently, closed my eyes and forced my mind to focus on the solution instead of the problem.

"Where are you?"

"At May's Café, Route 62, Cornudas."

"On the way to Fort Bliss?"

"Yes."

"Tell me what happened."

"Harry, we have to *do* something! I don't know where she is! The state she's in, she could do anything!"

I closed my eyes and enunciated each word, holding back the mounting anger. "Tell-me-what-happened!"

"We were exhausted, Mom needed the bathroom, so did Heather, and we needed gas. There's nothing between Hope and Fort Bliss until you get to Cornudas. So Dad said we'd pull in there, fill up, go to the john, buy some food and then press on till Phoenix."

"So what happened, Maggie?"

"I'm telling you, dammit!" She took a deep breath. "Mom went to the can. We ordered coffee and pancakes. Mom came back and Heather went to the john. The breakfast came and we were like halfway through when Mom says, 'Where's Heather?'"

"How long had passed?"

"I don't know. Maybe ten or fifteen minutes."

"Had you filled up?"

"*What?*"

"Had you already filled up with gas, Maggie?"

"Yes! What's that got to do with...? Oh."

"I'm assuming she took the car. She did take the car, right?"

"Yes."

"And you're stranded at Cornudas. Did you see which direction she took?"

"No. By the time we noticed she was long gone."

"Yeah, but it's a fair guess she went back to the studio."

She was quiet for a moment. "Yes, I guess so."

"I'll go and get her. How long ago did this happen?"

"Ten minutes ago, I guess. I called you almost straight away. Harry, I am sorry."

"Don't waste time on that now. So she has maybe twenty minutes' lead on us. She'll be driving fast. She could be there in the next fifteen minutes."

"What should we do?"

"Wait there. Don't move. I'll be with you within the hour."

I stood under a cold shower for three minutes and then got dressed. It was a slow and painful process. I pulled on my boots, and that was even slower and more painful. I figured it was already too late for me to get to the studio before Heather. And I knew enough about junkies, even if they were unwilling junkies, to know that the first thing she was going to do was find the heroin and get a fix. Whether she had bought cigarettes at Cornudas or a syringe at a drugstore, I had no idea. But what I was sure about was that I was going to arrive too late to stop her. My real problem was going to be what to do with her once I had her. Because come hell or high water, I had to be here when Oz arrived. The Oz story ended here, today.

But before that there was the more immediate problem of two smashed-up trucks and eight dead bodies blocking the road right outside the studio. By now the place would be crawling with firemen and deputies. If they took Heather into custody, we could have a major problem on our hands.

I made my way painfully down the stairs and checked my watch. Cornudas was about thirty miles from Dell City, about thirty-five from the studio. The road wasn't fantastic, but it was good enough and she could easily do sixty most of the way. Maggie had called me fifteen minutes earlier, and she'd put Heather's disappearance twenty minutes before that. Heather would be arriving at the studio about now. What she would find there was anybody's guess.

I grabbed the keys from the kitchen, took a slug of cold coffee and made my way out to the yard, where the Land Rover was waiting. There was nothing I could do about Oz, except get this done as fast as possible. If the deputies had already left the scene, I could lock Heather in the hangar, tell Maggie where she was, and return to deal with Oz. If the deputies were still there, I'd have to pray for inspiration, or better still a miracle.

I locked the door and walked across the dirt. Above me there was a flash of juddering light and the sky tore open. The crash of thunder made me duck. That was when I saw the vehicle on the road. It drew level with the driveway. As I watched I saw it enter the track and accelerate as it approached the Farm.

Pretty soon I saw it was a Ford pickup. It slowed, moved through the gate, and pulled up beside the Land Rover. The driver's door opened and Maggie climbed out. I felt the blood drain from my face and a hot, sick feeling in my gut. Maggie had taken her dad's Chevy, and Heather had taken it to go to the studio. This Ford I recognized. It was the only other truck that hadn't been totaled in the convoy that night. It was the truck Oz had used to escape.

She stood there beside the open door, under the black, bellying clouds, staring at me across fifteen feet of dust that might as well have been a million miles of deep space. The passenger door opened and Bill swung down, and Hanna climbed out behind him. I didn't need to ask. I realized now, too late, what had been wrong when I had spoken to Maggie on the phone. There was only one gas station in miles around, and Oz had told me a little while earlier that he was going to get gas. He had seen them. He had been watching them while I spoke to him. And now he was here to claim his ransom. There was no doubt in my mind what that ransom would be. It would not be one single thing. It would be the ledger, the two million in cash, my total humiliation, and then the lives of the four of us. Nothing less would satisfy him.

The far rear door opened and I watched his bald head as he came slowly around the back of the vehicle. He leaned his elbow on the tailgate. He had a semiautomatic in his hand.

He gave a short laugh and shook his head.

"You sure made one hell of a mess of the Farm. You done that all on your own. I salute you, yes sir. Reeee-spect! I managed to rescue a couple of pistols. Nothin' much else."

He looked at Maggie and her parents. "Oh," he said in mock surprise, holding up the weapon. "But this is just in case of an emergency. I do not intend to use it on either of these three beautiful people. When the time comes to kill them, I will do it with my hands, squeezing, beating and breaking."

I said, "That's not necessary."

His smile was almost urbane. "Who said anything about necessary? I am talking about pleasure."

"You want the ledger."

He nodded and waggled his eyebrows. "Yes please."

"You hurt these people and you will never see it as long as you live." He raised the weapon and aimed it at Bill's head. I spoke real fast. "I will give you the ledger. I'll show you where it is. You let them go and once they're safe you get the ledger, the money and the dope."

He frowned. "You have the dope too?"

I snorted. "What do you think?"

He seemed to think about it. "See," he said. "I don't think you take me seriously."

"I take you *very* seriously."

He shook his head. "No, I don't think you *respect* me."

"Oz, I could not respect you less if you were a pile of rat shit. But I do take you very seriously, and I am prepared to go to great lengths to give you what you want."

His eyes creased and he bent double as he emitted a high-pitched laugh. "Man! You are so scared! If you could see your face right now!" He laughed a little more. "It seems such a shame."

He strolled a few steps until he was standing behind Maggie and Hanna. "It seems such a *shame*, to have gone to all the trouble of bringing them here, only to let them go."

I turned and pointed toward the large barn in back of the house. "There's a drum of gasoline in that barn, Oz. Your ledger is sitting on top of it, your money, your heroin and your coke are stacked around it, and it has half a pound of C4, the same plastic explosive that killed your boys last night, stuck to its side. On a signal from my phone the C4 will explode, taking your ledger, your money and your dope with it." He watched me carefully. I went on, "Now, let's see if you take *me* seriously. Experience should tell you that that would be a good idea. Touch Maggie, her mother or Bill—just look at them like you intend to—and I will blow your dope, your money and your ledger into the stratosphere. After that I will come after you with what's left of the C4, I will stuff it down your throat and spread you all over New Mexico."

He nodded slowly. "OK, Harry, let's see it."

"No, you let them go. This is between you and me. You let them go, then we talk." He didn't do anything. He didn't say anything. He didn't even blink. I smiled. "Big talk. How did it go, Oz?" I mimicked his voice, "'I only got my arm cut, and I enjoy pain. You got your belly cut open, and you're burned out, and you don't enjoy pain. So I don't need anybody. I'm gonna drive down there, I am gonna beat you to a pulp, and then I am gonna gut you and hang you from your own fuckin' intestines.'"

He didn't like that and his face showed it. I laughed out loud. "Looks like in the end you did need somebody, Oz. You needed Maggie and her parents, because you were too chicken shit to face an injured man alone."

He nodded a few times. "I'm chicken shit?" He took another step forward. "*I'm* chicken shit?"

I knew too late I had pushed too far and too hard. His hand lashed out like a viper and the butt of his semiautomatic crashed into the back of Bill's head. He sprawled forward and fell face down in the dust. The blood seeping into his wispy hair was thick and flowing freely.

It was a fraction of a second. I was already moving, but Hanna was on him, attacking him from behind, clawing at his face with her nails. Maggie was screaming, running to her father. Oz spun, lashing out. My legs were like lead, dragging, heavy and slow. I was bellowing at him to stop, but my voice seemed to be echoing in a void where nobody could hear it. The back of his fist connected with her jaw, she staggered and fell. He took a step forward, leveling his weapon at her head. I jumped, felt a wrenching pain in my gut as I drove my right foot into his chest. There was an explosion. The semiautomatic jumped. I heard screams. I landed driving my fist into his face. His nose and mouth erupted in blood and he staggered back. I turned as though in slow motion and saw the sky light up with sheet lightning. In its shuddering glow I saw Maggie flinging herself across her mother. I saw the blood in the sand, and an insane, hot rage swelled in my head. Oz was stumbling backward, away from me, spitting blood and teeth—and laughing.

My roar was drowned out by the immense clap of thunder. I felt my belly clench like a fist and I sprang forward in a long, pendulum stride, pile-driving a side kick to his head. At the same instant he thrust the semiautomatic at me and fired. He was still stumbling and the recoil threw him back. My kick grazed his face and he fell to the ground.

As I came down I stamped hard on his injured arm. He screamed and let go of the semiautomatic, but rolled away from me, struggling to his feet, grabbing a handful of sand. I angled around, so what breeze there was was in his face. Then I lunged, lashing out a front kick at his knee. He took the kick with a snarl and as I drove a straight lead at his face, he weaved and powered a right hook into my wound.

In that moment I knew I was going to die. All my strength morphed into pain and drained out through my belly. I staggered back and he came after me swinging his huge fists like rocks. I weaved away from his left, but the right pounded into my ribs and I felt my legs going. I jabbed at his jaw but I had no strength or speed. It grazed his chin and his left uppercut drove through my guard, caught me on the side of the head and hurled me on my back.

The black sky above me rocked and spun. Gigantic millipedes

of light scuttled across the inky sky. Heaven roared, the universe crashed and the sky splintered. I lay on my back, unable to get up. Waves of nausea moved up from my gut into my head. I could feel my strength ebbing away in the sapping, humid heat.

Oz loomed over me, leering. Huge pellets of rain dropped out of the sky above him. I saw him snarl and grit his yellow teeth. His boot rose and he stamped at my belly. I got my arm in the way in time, but still the pain was more than you could believe possible.

Through the shards of agony in my head I was aware of the cool water cascading over my body, and I saw Oz turn and move away. Dimly in my mind I realized he was going for the semiautomatic. Something that was more than human made me roll on my side in the mud, with my hair matted over my face. A strength I did not possess, but possessed me, made me get to my feet. Wiping the water from my eyes, I saw Bill lying motionless, face down in the mud. I saw Hanna, lying on her back with her blood soaking into the growing puddles, and Maggie thrown over her, weeping, crying a single word over and over, "*No, no, no...*"

And I saw Oz stoop and reach for the weapon. He turned, the rain running down his bald head, and sneered at me as I lurched forward. He laughed and turned again, this time toward Maggie, and he raised the pistol. "Three for three!" he shouted, as the thunder rumbled above him.

The noise that came from inside me was not human. I screamed, and all the black, desert storm screamed with me. He was maybe nine or ten feet away. I was not aware of my feet touching the ground. I moved, rushing mindless at him through the downpour, fueled by a rage that my aching body could not suppress. I saw him look at me with crazy eyes and swing the weapon round the way he had done before. But before he could fire, my boot smashed into his hip. And before my boot had hit the ground, my right fist crashed into his ear, and a left hook pounded into his already bloody nose and mouth. As his arms went up to protect his face, a right hook drove up deep into his floating ribs, and he fell to his knees.

His eyes looked up at me through the bloody mess of his face. I knew my next kick, to his chin, would break his neck and kill him. In that instant he raised the gun to my face. Above me, the heavens ripped apart, the black deluge was flooded with violet and blue shuddering light and the sky exploded with extreme violence.

His eyes stayed on mine. Slowly he lowered the weapon. I could hear my own breathing rasping in my throat. There was a ringing that seemed to echo in my ears, silencing my thoughts, numbing my mind. I was acutely aware of the infinite, black flatness of the infernal world around me. My legs trembled and I reached out, trying not to fall. The rain was thundering down, saturating the flat clay. I could hear Maggie crying. Her mother was motionless. Bill was motionless.

In front of me, Oz dropped his weapon. His eyes glazed and he sagged sideways into the mud. In his side there was a large, ugly stain of thick, red blood that was spreading. It made no sense, but after a moment I looked to my right. Twenty feet away there was a Chevy, and the wipers were squeaking, batting furiously. In front of the Chevy, fifteen feet away, drenched, with strands of sodden hair clinging to her face, was Heather, holding a 9mm Glock in her hands.

EIGHTEEN

I CLIMBED IN THE CHEVY, OUT OF THE DOWNPOUR, AND pulled my cell from my pocket. I called the brigadier. It rang once as the rain drummed on the metal roof.

"Harry. Is it done?"

"Yes and no."

"Don't be cryptic."

"He has a nine-millimeter slug in his chest. I didn't put it there, but he must not die yet."

There was silence. "Explain."

I growled, "No. Get a cleanup team here. I need an ambulance and I need..."

"I thought you had understood..."

I roared, *"Well think again! You get a team here or you are going to have more fucking trouble on your hands than you know what to do with, sir!"*

There was a moment's silence. Then, very quiet, "Are you threatening me, Harry?"

"No, but if I have to I will. This situation is badly out of control. There are two civilians, good people, who are badly injured and there are a lot of people dead. I am injured, possibly seriously, and Oz is dying. We cannot let him die yet. And while we are talking, time is passing, and if the sheriff gets here and finds this mess, you are going to be explaining your ass to a Congressional Committee. So get me a *fucking team!*"

"All right. Where are you?"

I told him. "But you need to understand something, sir. There was a farm where they lived, on the Vazquez Hope Road, just outside Vazquez, that has been razed to the ground and the cops must be investigating that. There's what he called Studio Four, well camouflaged in a canyon in the Big Ridge, six miles directly east of the Farm. That is intact and you, or the Feds, need to get a team in there. Then there is the old studio, in the sand bowl beyond the fields on Williams Road, east of Dell City. There is a lot of heroin and coke buried there, there are two damaged trucks and there are a lot of bodies. This is spread over two counties in two states. If the sheriffs' departments are not too motivated, they'll probably buy that there has been some kind of gang warfare. But there is a lot of cleaning up to be done, and you'd better get your friends in the FBI onside."

"You have killed how many men, Harry?"

"About thirty."

"And none of them was Oz."

"I told you. I need him. We are not done here." He grunted. I went on. "And another thing, he abducted a woman, a young doctor with a promising career in San Diego. He made her a junkie and almost destroyed her. She is the one who put the slug in his side. She needs help. She cannot stand trial for this."

He sighed. "Understood. Do what you can for the injured. We'll get a team to you ASAP, and a couple of ambulances."

"But Oz comes home with me."

He was quiet. "Where?"

"Phoenix."

"OK, I'll see what I can do."

I hung up and sat staring through the rain-drenched windshield. Heather and Maggie were gone. I climbed out of the car and went to kneel beside Hanna. She was alive but she was unconscious and her breath was a fragile quiver. I looked up as her daughters emerged running from the house carrying blankets. For a moment I wondered if everybody was dead and they were going to cover them. They spread out a blanket beside Hanna and Heather snapped at me: "You know first aid?"

"Yes, of course."

"Help me get her on the blanket. One, two, three!" We lifted her on. "Now help me carry her inside. Maggie, see to Dad."

We made a hammock of the blanket and carried her carefully through the steady downpour inside, where we laid her on the sofa.

"Help Maggie bring Dad in while I see to Mom."

I went out into the sun again. The world rocked a couple of times but I managed to get to Maggie. She glanced up at me. Her hair and her face were drenched.

"I think he's alive."

I checked and his pulse was strong. "He's OK. Let's get him inside."

We rolled him onto the blanket as we had done with Hanna and between us carried him to the living room where we laid him on the floor with cushions under his head. I said to Heather, "There is an ambulance coming."

"How long?"

"I'm not sure."

"The bullet has pierced her left side. I have no equipment. If I try to remove it I might cause a hemorrhage." She was fighting hard to keep it together. "But if I don't do something soon…"

I spoke automatically, like it wasn't me but a program drummed into me over long years.

"Make a field dressing, stop the bleeding, keep her hydrated. You also need to get them both dry and warm."

She glanced at me and nodded, then went to get the stuff we had used earlier in the kitchen. To Maggie I said, "I can't let Oz die yet."

There was rage in her eyes when she looked at me. "What?"

"There are people behind him. I need them."

"This has to stop."

"Explain that to the kids. You're going to save your parents. Who's going to save the next bunch of kids they bring in from Mexico, or the Ukraine?"

She left and went upstairs. She came down a moment later with a sheet and I followed her out into the steady rain where Oz was lying motionless in a pool of bloody rain. Lightening crackled across the sky. I felt his pulse. It was weak, but not as weak as Hanna's.

He was heavy. We rolled him onto the sheet and, with great difficulty, dragged him toward the house. We left him on the floor with a cushion under his head, and I applied a field dressing to his wound to stem the flow of blood. There was nothing more I could do.

I stood. Heather was washing the wound on her father's head.

"Heather?" She glanced at me. "Help is coming."

"I'm just cleaning the wound."

"I don't mean that. I mean for everyone. It's going to be OK."

She nodded and turned back to her father. I walked into the kitchen. There was a deep, unnatural ache in all my limbs, and I could feel my heart racing. I went to the door and leaned on the jamb. Thunder split the sky and threatened to tear the house in half. I lifted my shirt and looked. The bandage Maggie had applied was saturated with blood, but not all of it had come from the torn stitches beneath it. A good deal had come from the neat hole that had been put through it by the 9mm slug Oz had pumped through me.

I opened the door and stood looking at the storm. Two enormous black birds hovered in the sky beneath the bellying clouds. They looked like giant vultures. I knew they were coming to get me. I could see them closing in and turning, staring down and searching with their huge, glowing eyes. They engulfed me and I was gone.

. . .

I AWOKE to the feeling of a cool breeze on my face. I was in a large room that had a Spanish feel to it: white walls, heavy wooden beams supporting the ceiling, a heavy, oak wardrobe across the room, a couple of heavy wood and leather chairs. To my right a window stood open and lace curtains moved slightly in the cool air. Outside the sky was very blue, but the window was in the shade of tall trees. I could hear the leaves whispering, and there was the sound of birds and water. It was not a pool, it sounded more like a fountain, or a stream.

Absently, my hands found clean bandages around my waist, and gauze and sticking plaster on my left cheek.

I tried to sit, but the knitting needles in my belly told me that wasn't such a good idea. So I eased myself up, first on my elbow and then carefully around into a sitting position. A small brass bell sat on the old, Castilian bedside table. I sat a moment in peace and quiet, thinking how nice it was not to have to talk to the brigadier or the colonel. The birds and the water seemed to make a lot more sense than they did right then.

So I sat like that for a while, enjoying the peace and, for some reason, remembering the smell of honeysuckle. That reminded me of Maggie and after another while I sighed and rang the bell.

A couple of minutes passed and there was a tap at the door. I made a fair imitation of a toad and the colonel must have understood because she opened the door. She was not in uniform. She was in jeans and a white blouse, with her hair pulled back into a loose ponytail. She looked cool and relaxed, and nice to watch. She smiled and pulled up one of the heavy chairs. As she sat she said, "And you were doing so well."

"Wasn't I? How could it all go so wrong?"

"You are not the only person asking that question."

"I can give you a clue." She smiled a little more, not particularly in a nice way, raised her eyebrows and nodded. I took that as a go ahead. "Send one, unsupported man against a psychopathic feudal king with a psychopathic army of over thirty well-armed men in a fortress with not one, but two electrified fences, Rottweilers and *two* studios where he makes snuff movies and traffics large amounts of class-A drugs, and chances are things will stop going well. You know *why* that can make things go wrong?"

"Is this a trick question?"

"Your one, unsupported man is going to have to get pretty extreme, simply to get close enough to the psychotic feudal king to throw bombs at him, let alone quietly stab him with a stiletto."

"You took the job, Harry."

"The job had to be done, Jane. But unless you start running a work experience program for the Royal College of Ninjas in Japan, this kind of job is always going to be messy."

She nodded for a bit, looking at the floor. "Messy..."

I smiled on the bandaged side of my face. "What, it wasn't messy?"

She held my eye a moment. "It was messy."

I shrugged. "Like I said."

She nodded a few more times, holding my eye. "You killed thirty men or more, whom you were not sent to kill, and you did not kill Oz..."

She trailed off. I smiled sweetly. "You didn't finish the sentence, Colonel. I killed thirty men I was *not* sent to kill and failed to kill the one man I *was* sent to kill. Oops! You didn't send me to kill him." She didn't answer but she did hold my eye. I went on. "I killed thirty men or more in self-defense. I could have killed Oz, but I chose not to, yet, because we need him."

"We?"

"Yes, we."

"In what way, under what bizarre interpretation of the universe, does Cobra need Oscar Larsen?"

"Has either of you read the ledger?"

"Not yet. You have kept us pretty busy talking to various government departments."

"Read it, and then I'll tell you why *we* need Oz Larsen."

"Yeah, well, meantime, you were shot, twice."

"I gathered. Once in the gut and once in the face. Unless this is next week, I gather neither shot did much damage."

She took a deep breath through her nose and closed her eyes a moment. "I came up here telling myself I was not going to get mad at you. You were *shot*, Harry, with a 9mm semiautomatic at close range."

"Is this next week? How long have I been asleep?"

"Twelve hours."

"And you still haven't read the ledger?" She sagged back in her chair. I said, "I'm serious. That ledger is very important."

"We have had other things to do. Like clean up the almighty mess you left behind. Let me tell you that the Texas Rangers were not amused when they were told the case was being taken over at a federal level."

"I bet. Now, you and the brigadier need to read it. Second, I have been out for just twelve hours, if this had been major surgery I'd be drooling and telling you how much you mean to me. I'm not, so it wasn't major surgery. The slug in my belly missed my intestines and simply tore the muscle. The one in my face scorched my cheek and will do no more than leave me with an interesting scar. These are not problems. Oz is a problem. Where is he?"

"Locked in a room and handcuffed to the bed."

"He'll like that."

She didn't seem very amused. "He was shot by a civilian. Not you."

I felt a hot flush of anger in my belly. "I am injured and unwell, you should not make me angry. He was shot by a woman whom he had abducted, enslaved and made into a junkie. He was shot by a woman who had a promising career as a doctor ahead of her. He was shot by a woman whose parents were lying in the mud bleeding to death."

She nodded. "I know. We have debriefed her and her sister."

"Did Hanna and Bill make it?"

She raised an eyebrow. "Hanna and Bill?"

I felt the anger hot and fast again. "Yeah, Hanna and Bill, those are their names. They are people, with names." I knew what she was thinking and I sat forward, pointing at her despite the pain. "You're thinking I got too personally involved. But you're overlooking the fact that this was not an official, political hit. This was you and me and the brigadier getting personally involved in the fact that this bastard was walking away from a trial on a technicality. So, no, I did not *get* personally involved. I *was* personally involved, and so were you and so was the brigadier!"

"OK, but the brigadier is going to want to know why Oz was still alive and at large and in a position to threaten the lives of this family."

"Yeah? He is going to want to know that? Good, because I am going to tell him, in detail. And I will tell him, and you, something else. And I'll tell you for nothing. What I did out there in that hellhole, neither you nor him could do on steroids! So put that in your smug pipe and smoke it."

"OK."

"Stop saying, 'OK,' like that. Where is the brigadier? Why isn't he here? And where are the Joneses? Are they OK?"

"They're OK. Mrs. Jones is out of danger, so is Mr. Jones, though he has a fearful headache. Heather has voluntarily put herself into a rehabilitation program, and Maggie...," she raised an eyebrow at me, "is running around like a..."

She was momentarily at a loss for a simile so I offered her, "A blue-assed fly?"

"...*what?*"

I sank back against the cushions. "The Brits used to say it in the Regiment. Only they said 'arse' or 'arsed.' Running around like a blue-arsed fly."

"What the hell is a blue-arsed fly?"

"A fly with a blue ass, Colonel. A bluebottle, *calliphora vomitoria*. They never stop, they are constantly on the go," I moved my finger around in the air, "bzzz, bzzzz."

"Good lord. Yes, she is running around like a blue-arsed fly, being universally helpful and charming, in that Deep South way."

"Great. Do I have to make an appointment to see the brigadier so he can chew me out, or will the next ten minutes be OK?"

"He asked me to come up and see how you were. If you are up to it, he'd like to see you." She stood. "Harry?"

"What?"

"He was worried about you."

I didn't know what to answer, so I said, "Oh."

"So was I."

"Thanks. I was OK."

"So I see."

We stayed like that for a moment, in silence. Finally I said, "You going to help me shower and get dressed?"

She frowned. "No!"

"You want to leave, then, so I can do it by myself?"

She sighed and left and closed the door a little more forcefully than was perhaps necessary.

NINETEEN

I FOUND THEM, AS USUAL, OUT BY THE POOL AT A TABLE in the shade of a large parasol. The brigadier was, uncharacteristically, in jeans with a checked shirt that had the sleeves rolled up. One of the brigadier's many firm beliefs was that men did not wear short-sleeved shirts. Little boys wore short-sleeved shirts, men rolled up their sleeves. Personally I thought that was stupid, but I had never been able to wear a short-sleeved shirt since he'd said it.

Men wore their sleeves rolled up.

He watched me approach, through heavy, black sunglasses, and as I sat he said, "How are you? Are you coping with the pain?"

I winced as I settled myself. "What pain?"

He gave a small grunt that said he wasn't impressed. Trying to impress an Englishman of the brigadier's class with your stoicism is like taking a cool box to Antarctica to keep your beers cold.

"I suppose you're bound to feel a little discomfort for a while. Would you like a drink?"

I nodded. "Yeah, I could use a pint of Guinness."

The colonel stood. "I'll get it. Alex?"

"Whisky and soda, please, Jane."

She left and the brigadier took a deep breath. "Harry, I am a little bit at a loss. I have a great deal of respect for you as an operative and a soldier, and please don't think I am criticizing you, but what the *fuck* happened?"

I arched my eyebrows. I have to say I am not easily shocked, but when the brigadier started using four-letter words, that was the time to start looking for five-legged purple cows and flying pigs.

"I mean," he went on, "I thought we had set the parameters very clearly. Kill him, be discreet, you are on your own, and do not involve Cobra." He sighed again. "Now, what did you do? You caused two explosions, one of them the size of Hiroshima, you involved a whole family of civilians, scattered bodies quite literally all over two counties and two states, called on Cobra to come and clean up the mess, and, to cap it all, *you did not kill the target!*" He crossed one leg over the other, made a temple of his fingers and frowned. "I repeat, what the *fuck* happened?"

I scratched my head and sighed. "Well, sure, you put it like that..."

"Please, Harry, don't retreat into facetious cockiness. We know each other well enough for you to be honest. You are Cobra's best operative, I am asking you please to explain how this disaster happened."

I nodded. "OK, well, for a start it was never going to work, and we should all have seen that from the start. Second," I spread my hands, "even if it wasn't going to work, it had to be done. So what we should have foreseen from the beginning was that we were always going to have a situation on our hands at the end of it. Why?"

I shrugged at my own rhetorical question. "First because Oz was hiding behind an army of devoted psychopaths, within a fortress that was extremely well guarded. Second, he and his followers did not give a damn about being discreet. They were aggressively predatory and trusted implicitly that they could do whatever they liked in Manuel Vazquez County. Not least because they owned the sheriff, and the sheriff was all the law enforcement the county had. Third..."

I heard movement behind me and a moment later the colonel set down a tray of chilled Guinness on the table. We toasted and I drained half my glass. I sighed, wiped my mouth with the back of my hand and continued.

"Third, on the night I arrived, four of Oz's boys came to the Jones's hotel, where I was staying, looking for Mrs. Jones, intending to rape her in front of her husband. Once they were finished, they were going to go looking for the daughter, Maggie. Considering I was there to kill Oz for doing precisely that kind of thing, I didn't feel I could turn a blind eye. Hell," I gave a short laugh, "even if I could have, I didn't want to, and I wouldn't. Mainly because I am a human being." I paused a moment. "You know what Bruce Lee said?"

He raised an eyebrow. "I know you're going to tell me."

"He said that Jeet Kune Do was the art of honestly expressing yourself. You can put on a show, be cocky, blind yourself with your own show, but to express yourself honestly, without lying to yourself, that, my friend, is very hard to do."

"Your point?"

"I honestly expressed myself. If I had not protected that family that night, I would have been a liar and a hypocrite, and my presence there, for the purpose of killing Oz, would have been a sham. So I honestly expressed myself and killed those four boys, and threw them in the Guadalupe River."

"And it was that self-expression that triggered all the following events."

"Pretty much. There is one other reason this all went south."

"And what's that?"

"Oz is a very, very dangerous man. He is unpredictable, totally uninhibited and very strong. Not just physically, but internally, in his motivation. He is the dark side of honestly expressing yourself. There is no hypocrisy about him. He is what he is. And he very nearly killed me."

The colonel smiled. "I believe you owe your life to Heather. Isn't that the second woman you owe your life to now?"

I observed her through hooded eyes. "The only woman I owe my life to is my mother. I was about to break his neck with a front kick when Heather shot him. So the job is not done yet, and I have to kill him."

"Yes, there is something I am not clear about, Harry, in spite of your very enlightening narrative. He was lying, moribund, in the mud, with a bullet in his gut. Why did you not simply confirm the kill?"

I sighed. "You haven't read the ledger."

He echoed my sigh. "No, Jane told me you have been banging on about the ledger."

"Banging on?" I smiled and shook my head. "You really need to read that ledger, sir. I am not done with Oz, and *you* need to know what's in that ledger before I tell you what I intend to do."

I drained the Guinness and stood. "I am going to find a spot to do some qui gong exercises. Meantime let me leave you with this thought. Have you ever heard of Abdul ben Elahi?"

They glanced at each other and shook their heads. The brigadier answered. "No, who is he?"

"I was reminded of him at Cobra HQ when you were telling me about Oz. Among other things, he ran master classes online, teaching aspiring pedophiles how to obtain pornographic pictures of kids without getting caught. Basically, his technique was this: you target families who are in serious debt, who risk losing their homes and having their kids go into care. You promise them money in exchange for some harmless videos or photographs, and then you blackmail them with the threat of exposure if they don't take photos and record videos of serious child abuse.

"When he was caught, he had a network of two thousand

victims worldwide. Well, this bastard, who is now in prison, from where we all know he continues to operate, was, and is still, Oz's partner." I nodded. "There's more. Oz has *a lot* of partners who help him evade the law and stay one step ahead of arrest and conviction. But, as I keep banging on, you need to read the ledger."

"Fine." He sat forward and knocked the table with his knuckles, like he was summoning action. "An hour and a half and we rendezvous here for lunch. Good for you?"

This was addressed to the colonel, who nodded without looking at me. I hobbled away to look for somewhere quiet and shaded where I could curl up and die. I found a small fountain in the shade of a eucalyptus grove and there spent the next hour doing breathing exercises and slow, gentle movements, trying to persuade my body it was a good idea to get strong again. My body didn't seem to be all that convinced.

By the time I had finished my stomach had conceded at least that a sirloin steak and another Guinness might be a good idea. I was putting on my socks and boots when the brigadier appeared around the side of the house, carrying the ledger in his hand. He approached, crossed his ankles and lowered himself into a sitting position on the grass.

"All right," he said, "Judge Casper Williams, as you suspected in the beginning. Senator Geordi Bardolino..."

He paused and looked down at the grass in front of him. I continued, "Billionaire financier Walter de la Potesta, presidential advisor Mahmood Abadi, CEO of Global Holdings Kit Weiner..."

"Yes," he raised a hand, "yes, Harry, I have understood. There is no need to press the point. What I need to know—or perhaps what I need you to understand—is that this job, taking out Oz, *must be* an exception. It cannot signify the opening of the floodgates. That is precisely why we stressed to you from the beginning that Cobra could not be involved." He gave a small, humorless laugh and shook his head. "We cannot take it upon ourselves to start eliminating private citizens because we view them as criminals above the law."

"Isn't that what we already do?"

"No, in fact it is exactly what we stand against. What you have to understand, Harry, is that however much a man or a woman may *deserve* to be eliminated, we—you and I—are not entitled as members of Cobra to eliminate him. Because once you open that door, the lines between what can and cannot be done, what may and may not be done, begin to blur, and instead of eliminating the enemies of humanity, it becomes the powerful crushing the weak. We become our enemy."

I looked up at the dappled leaves and recited what Oz had said to me. "Good does not punish evil; evil is its own justitioner."

He nodded. "Yes. I am not sure justitioner is a word, but if it isn't it should be. We operate as soldiers, on a political stage, within strict limits and according to strict guidelines. We have, sitting here, identified five men, there are others mentioned in the ledger. Which ones are we going to kill? How do we decide which ones live? Cobra's guidelines are very strict: the target must have committed crimes against humanity as defined by the Geneva Convention. These men and women, however monstrous they might be, do not enter into that definition. So how do we decide who lives and who dies? And in making that decision, do *we* put ourselves into the category of committing crimes against humanity?"

I shook my head. "That is all too complicated for me, sir. What I see with great clarity is that we knew, in our bones, that Oscar Larsen had to die. What we did not know at the time, when we took that decision, was that he was not alone, and there were five other men who had to die with him, for exactly the same reasons that he had to die. Oz dies because he's a bastard and he is out there, upfront about the fact that he's a bastard. But the rats and the cockroaches and the snakes that hide behind a façade of respectability, who sit in judgment on others, and make laws, and shape public opinion, they don't have to die.

They get to live and prosper. That is not expressing oneself honestly."

"Honest expression or not, Harry, we cannot institute a program for murdering civilians."

"I am not proposing that."

"What are you proposing, then?"

"I'm proposing finishing the job we started."

"Killing Oz?"

"Yeah." I nodded. "Killing Oz, Judge Casper Williams, Senator Geordi Bardolino, Walter de la Potesta, Mahmood Abadi, Kit Weiner… and Abdul ben Elahi, all in one go."

He arched his eyebrows and sat up straight, like his eyebrows were trying to drag him up toward the sky.

"And how will you accomplish that? Not another bomb, please!" I drew breath to answer, but he raised a hand and said, "Wait, I think Jane should be part of this."

He leaned back and shouted her name a couple of times. She peered around the side of the house and he motioned her to come. I had a sudden, bizarre feeling I was in Sardinia or Umbria with my eccentric, Bohemian uncle and his young wife, and he wanted to show her an interesting pediment.

She sat between us and the brigadier said, "I want you to be part of this conversation, Jane. Harry believes he might be able to take out the five names we identified, plus Oscar Larsen and Abdul ben Elahi, all in one fell swoop."

She frowned at me. "How?"

"It has to be in two stages. The first stage is for Oz to set up a meeting with these five people."

"Is that possible?"

"Very much so. Oz has these people in his pocket. He owns them. They will have heard through the grapevine what has happened and it won't surprise them that he wants to touch them for something. They'll be expecting it. So we make the demand, but we also offer them a lure, something they really want."

"Like freedom from Larsen."

"Exactly. So he demands a meeting. They'll play hard to get at first, but they'll agree in the end. And we, directly or implicitly, put their release from blackmail on the table. Maybe we also offer some other cash or business benefit of interest to Oz, to make it more credible. He was aiming to retire to Brazil, so we can work with that."

The brigadier grunted. "OK, so you've got them together, what's part two?"

"I have to get them together in one room. I will pass myself off as his personal assistant. We are both injured after the recent fracas, so that will lend it credibility."

The colonel pressed me. "How do you plan to kill them? You can't just pull a gun and shoot them all. Besides, they won't want you present during the talks, that will be confidential between the six of them. Particularly the senator and the judge will want to keep it strictly to the cabal."

"Sure," I said, and smiled at her. "I intend to bring them together, give them a little talk, and then leave while they negotiate and make their deal."

The brigadier suppressed a sigh behind a polite smile. "So, at the risk of being repetitive, how do you plan to make the kill?"

"Well, here's the beauty of it," and I told them. When I had finished they sat in stunned silence. Eventually the colonel shook her head and looked at the brigadier. He avoided her eyes and looked up at the sky through the slender leaves of the eucalyptus.

"Harry," he said eventually, "I don't know. I honestly don't know. The risk element is very high."

I shrugged. "It's the only way to do it."

The colonel shook her head several times. "I think it's madness."

"Maybe it is madness," I said, "but the whole job was madness from the get-go. What is very clear is that the job has to be finished, and this is the only way to finish it."

The brigadier stood. "All right, let's have lunch, and take the afternoon to think about it. We'll make a decision over breakfast tomorrow."

I stood too, carefully, and smiled at the brigadier. Brigadier Alexander "Buddy" Byrd, even back in the Regiment, he never decided to launch an attack, or take out a position, or hit a target, unless some form of refreshment was involved. And now the decision to murder six men would be finally taken over breakfast. After all, I told myself, we are not savages, are we?

TWENTY

I OPENED THE DOOR AND STEPPED INTO OZ'S ROOM AT A quarter to twelve the next day. He was sitting in bed watching television, with his left hand handcuffed to the metal frame of the bed. I'd have been happier if both hands and both ankles had been chained to the bed, but I figured it was safe enough.

He watched me come in with mockery on his face and in his eyes.

"What's a guy got to do to get laid around here?"

"It can be arranged."

He looked surprised and laughed. "You're kidding. What do I have to do?"

I pulled up a chair on his right side, where he couldn't reach me if he decided to jump out of bed, and sat.

"What else do you want?"

"Huh?"

"Do you want your two million bucks returned? Do you want another eight million thrown in on top? Do you want to relocate to Brazil, with a new identity? Do you want your criminal record expunged? What do you want?"

"I want all that, and for the third fuckin' time, what do I have to do to get it?"

"Arrange a meeting."

"Arrange a meeting? Who with?"

"Judge Casper Williams, Senator Geordi Bardolino, Walter de la Potesta, Mahmood Abadi and Kit Weiner."

He threw back his head and roared with loud noisy laughter. "Man, you have got to be kidding!"

I stood. "OK, but let me leave you with a thought, Oscar. Do you know what they do to pedophiles in prison?"

Before I got to the door he was already saying, "OK, OK, OK, wait a minute, let's talk."

I stopped with my hand on the handle. "I don't want to talk to you, Oscar. I want to kill you, and I would gladly do it right now. If the next best thing is that you get beaten and tortured for the next fifteen or twenty years, I'll settle."

I turned the handle and watched him frown, and the first hint of panic in his eyes. I opened the door an inch and he said, "Wait."

"If you are willing to do exactly as I tell you, we can make you an offer. But make no mistake, Oscar. This is not a negotiation. There is an offer on the table which my superiors are reluctant to make. They want you dead, period. I want you dead too, so the dice are loaded against you from the start. Thing is, that ledger changed everything, and now I also want Williams, Geordi Bardolino, de la Potesta, Mahmood Abadi and Weiner. But that offer expires the minute I step out through that door. From that point on the countdown begins to the day in the shower or in the yard, or in your bed, when they stick you with a shiv."

"Jesus Christ, OK! I said OK!"

I closed the door and sat down again. "So, you must have some way of contacting these people."

He nodded. "Yeah. We have dedicated email accounts and we use BiP to message each other."

"So I need you to arrange a meeting."

"Where?"

"At the judge's house."

"He'll never go for that."

"Yes, he will, because you are going to tell them you want out. Things have got too hot. You want a new identity, you want ten million bucks and you want to relocate to Brazil. In exchange you give them the ledger and you leave them all off the hook. You will never see each other again. If they refuse, you will go to the Feds and hand over the ledger in exchange for immunity."

He thought about it, gazing out of the window for a while. He asked, absently, "So do I get ten mil from you and ten mil from them?"

"If, *if*, you get them to incriminate themselves."

He scowled and turned to look at me. "I'll be wearing a wire?"

"No, we'll be using other techniques. That doesn't concern you. All you need to do is make sure that each one of them makes some kind of statement to incriminate himself."

He studied me for a while.

"You've got the ledger. The Feds can confirm every entry in that book by checking financial and telephone records, as well as trips undertaken, hotels stayed at... What do you want this for?"

"I don't, they do. Because they thought they had you dead and buried, but you wriggled out. That is not going to happen this time. It has to be absolutely watertight."

He nodded, then shrugged. "Sure, why not. I'll sink 'em for you. I'll get them talkin'. It'll be easy. When do you want to do this?"

"In the next day or two." I grinned. "How are your ribs?"

"Fine, how're yours?"

"Mine are bruised. You have a powerful hook." I pointed at him. "But yours are fractured and cracked in three places. I've seen the X-rays they took while you were unconscious."

He waved a finger at me. "I told you, asshole, that you do not represent good, and you are not my justitioner. You did not bring me down, it was Heather, who is touched by evil."

"You're full of shit, Oz." There was a knock on the door and I opened it to see three nurses wheeling a trolley. Two were pretty and young, the third was big, male and as ugly as impure thoughts. I turned back to Oz. "And another thing, the word 'justitioner' does not exist."

"Does now," he said and ogled the nurses. "So, ladies, which part of me do you want to bandage first?"

I closed the door and left him with his fantasies.

THE NEXT DAY, with my belly swathed in clean bandages, the brigadier's assistants found Judge Casper Williams' telephone number and address and I called him at home. I told the woman who answered that I needed to discuss some urgent business with the judge, which concerned his friends Senator Geordi Bardolino, Walter de la Potesta, Mahmood Abadi and Kit Weiner.

She asked me to wait and I did, for a full five minutes. Then a gravelly, urbane voice came on the line.

"Who is this, please?"

"My name is Harry Field, you don't know me, sir. But I was recently in New Mexico where I witnessed some extraordinary events which I believe could be of interest to you and your associates."

His voice became patronizing, but he didn't hang up.

"What possible interest could I have in what you witnessed in New Mexico, Mr. Field?"

"It involved a couple of film studios, and a farm. The thing is, Judge, I am pretty sure it would be of interest not just to you, but as I said, to your friends."

"What friends are you talking about, Mr. Field?"

"You know, sir, Senator Geordi Bardolino, Kit Weiner, Walter de la Potesta... Should I go on? I mean, are you sure you want to have this conversation over the telephone? Wouldn't you prefer to have it in the privacy and security of your office?"

"No, we meet somewhere neutral..."

"No, chief. We meet in your office. We're going to talk for ten minutes. Then I leave and you never see me again. Believe me, you wanna hear what I have to tell you. I'll be there in twenty minutes."

I hung up and went down to the garage where I climbed into the dark blue Range Rover and took off through the Arizona mid-morning heat toward East Mockingbird Lane.

The house was vast and managed to look like a gaudy restaurant in a holiday resort that was all the rage twenty years ago. It had domes, copulas, terraces, hanging gardens, rambling gardens and formal Italianate gardens, all overshadowed by huge palm trees and framed by very well brought up lawns.

I buzzed at the gate and told them who I was and that I had an appointment with the judge. For a moment I thought they were going to tell me to go to hell, but the gate eventually buzzed open and I drove down the salmon pink drive to the sweeping, white marble steps that rose to the arched, arabesque doorway. It was like a thousand and one nights in Vegas.

There was a guy in an Italian, double-breasted suit at the door to meet me. He had an intimidating wire poking up out of his jacket and into his ear. I figured it kept him connected to the Hive Mind.

He said, "Follow me."

I followed him through a white marble hall with two sweeping caracole staircases, one on either side, curling in to meet either side of a statue of David. I wondered if this was the real one, and the one at the *Galleria dell'Accademia* in Florence was a copy.

The guy with the wire in his ear led me down several red-carpeted corridors until we came to a magnificent polished oak door upon which he knocked. He must have heard something I didn't because he opened the door and said, "Harry Field, sir."

After a moment he stepped back and let me in.

Judge Casper Williams was sitting behind a large oak desk with a green leather blotter, pretty much as you would expect him to be. He stared at me with hostile, pale blue eyes that sat at the top of a beaky nose and made him look like an outraged peregrine falcon.

"I won't ask you to sit down, Mr. Field, because you promised you would leave quickly and I would not see you again. Tell me what you want, then kindly leave."

I smiled on the un-bandaged side of my face and sat in the chair he hadn't offered me.

"I work for Oz," I said.

The blood drained from his face, leaving him looking like pale gray soot. He didn't say anything, so I went on, examining the room as I spoke.

"It's been a tough week for Oz, you know that?" Again he didn't answer so I looked him in the eye. "Did you know that, I'm askin'?"

"Yes, yes, I had heard something."

"It's a lot of damage. Son of a bitch destroyed the Farm, two studios, killed a lot of bros. Oz got shot. Did you know that?"

"Yes."

"See? I'm askin' you, did you know that? And you're sayin', 'Yeah, yeah, I knew that.' But you didn't send him chocolates, huh? You didn't send him flowers? You know, a guy like Oz, he's tough. He is as hard as fuckin' granite, man, but inside he has a heart, and he has feelings, and it upsets him when his friends don't come to him in a moment of need. Now I am gonna ask you, Judge, did you come to him in his moment of need?"

"Well, we were talking..."

"Talking?"

"We, we, we..." He swallowed hard. "We were discussing the best way to help him. We were not sure where he was—"

"He is right here in Phoenix."

"Here? *Here?* In Phoenix?"

"Is that a problem?"

"Of course not."

"So he is going to come and see you, and your pals the senator, Walt, Mahmood Weiner the wiener." I sat forward and leaned my elbows on the desk. "It would be a really *bad* idea if any of you were not to show up. I don't even want to think about what the consequences might be, for you and your family, for their families. So make yourselves available, Judge, and tell your friends that it is real important you are there for Oz, in his time of need." I frowned. "Am I getting through to you, Casper?"

"Yes."

"Because you have this stupid look on your face, like maybe you're shitting your pants and are finding it hard to focus on what I am saying to you."

Walt, Mahmood Weiner"I understand, and I will communicate with our friends to ensure that they are there."

"Good. That is very good. Ensure they're there. You have a way with words, Judge. You express yourself very eloquently. Ensure—they are there. I admire that in a man."

I stood, applauding myself silently on my performance, and looked hard into the judge's eyes. "I'm a killer, Judge, you know that, don't you?"

He nodded. I echoed the nod. "Good. I am going to leave now, but I will be back. In the meantime, when Oz calls, cooperate with him. Make it easy for him, and maybe, just maybe, in a couple of months all of this will be just like a bad dream."

He swallowed again with difficulty and nodded once. "Yes, I understand."

OVER THE NEXT twenty-four hours or so the brigadier and I worked with Oz, in the brigadier's office at the back of the house, on an exchange of messages with the judge, the senator, Walter de la Potesta, Mahmood Abadi and Kit Weiner. All of the messages, and their replies, were recorded onto a Cobra computer and sent to the Cobra mainframe. In addition the entire exchange was filmed.

At first the responses from the five men were predictable, evasive, trying to distance themselves from Oz and persuade him it was unwise to meet until things cooled down. However, his reply to the senator late in the evening of the second day—copied to all five men—brought them to attention.

Either you talk to me now, or I talk to my friends at North 7th Street.

There was a protracted silence, then the judge wrote:

What is that supposed to mean?

I'm through. I want out. So either we talk terms, or I take my ledger to the FBI and tell them everything in exchange for immunity. There is everything they could possibly want in here, gentlemen. Everything: dates, accounts, services, payments. Every single one of you motherfuckers will be traced and sent down. So, if you don't wanna talk to me, I know somebody who does.

Wait.

It was the judge. After a minute he came back.

Where and when?

Tomorrow afternoon, three PM at your house on Mockingbird Lane. And I want every damn one of you there. If I walk in and don't see five fuckin' faces looking at me, I leave and you are all dead. IS THAT CLEARLY UNDERSTOOD?

Yes, just relax, will you?

What do you want?

He looked at me. I said, "Money and out."

Money and out.

How much?

We discuss that tomorrow.

And what do we get in exchange?

I said, "Wait. Tell them they are in no position to try to negotiate terms. But you are prepared to give them the ledger."

You motherfuckers ain't in no position to make demands, asshole! You get whatever I give you. But you accommodate me, and I will hand over the ledger. We draw a line under this thing and I disappear.

He looked at me and I nodded. He pressed send. A moment later the reply came back:

OK, we'll be there. But you have to understand there is a limit to what we can do.

Four more messages popped up from the other four members of the cabal confirming they would be there. For good measure Oz added:

Show up and pay up. One of you fails, you all go down. Just make sure you're there.

HE LOOKED from the brigadier to me and back again. His movements were awkward because of the plaster cast he had fitted around his body to try and immobilize his broken ribs. His arms stuck out and made him look like a toy robot.

"So I done good," he said. "I'm on my way to becoming a reformed citizen. How about you gentlemen let me out for the night? You know you got me. You know it's in my interest to come back. I just *need* a beer, a whiskey, a sweet bit of..."

"Can it, Larsen. I wouldn't trust you to piss on yourself if you were on fire. Tomorrow afternoon you can do whatever the hell you like. The moment you walk into that meeting and get them to talk, you are a free man."

His big ugly face creased into a stupid grin.

"Until then," I said, "You remain chained to your bed watching reruns of *The Muppets.*"

He curled his lip. "I am going to arrange for a special place in hell for you, Harry. You'll have to watch *Little House on the Prairie* on a loop for the rest of eternity."

"Come on, get up!" I tipped his chair and he got awkwardly to his feet. "Be grateful I haven't got you in a cellar removing your digits with pliers, you son of a bitch."

I shoved him toward the door and we took him upstairs to his room where he was handcuffed to the bed again and locked in with the TV. Maybe he settled in to watch repeats of *Little House on the Prairie*, or *The Waltons.*

TWENTY-ONE

THE COLONEL WAS BESIDE THE POOL NURSING A TALL gin and tonic. The moon was in the pool, warping, stretching, occasionally breaking up, watching us with a sly eye. I sat and the brigadier emerged from what he called the drawing room with a tray of whisky, gin, tonic and ice.

I sat and he poured. I said, "Where are Hanna and Bill?"

"At the Lincoln, but it would be very unwise for you to go and see them. You could put them at risk."

He handed me my drink and I sipped while he poured himself a dram.

"What about Heather?"

"The Ian Fraser Kilmister Memorial. Again, Harry, you would not be doing her any favors..."

"I know. What about Maggie?"

He sighed and sat. The colonel asked, "Why do you want to know, Harry?"

"I want to know." I looked at her for a moment, feeling unreasonably angry. I shifted my gaze to the lying moon, lying in the pool, always whispering lies, always hiding in ethereal turquoise. "They stood up to be counted. They didn't have to. But they were there and they didn't back down, not one of them. They stood up for each other, as a family, but they stood up for me too.

"I know the best thing I can do for them, is leave them alone." My voice came out more bitter than I intended, but I went on. "I'd just like them to know that I didn't turn my back on them. That I give a damn, and I'm not just walking away."

The brigadier said, half to himself, "It's what you should do," and I let the ambiguity stand.

For a while the only sound was the turquoise lapping of the pool. Until the colonel said, "Apparently," and her voice was startling in the quiet, "I have discovered recently, that many people would rather have slightly shorter lives, if that means spending what time they have with the people they love.[1]"

I snorted. "Who knew?"

The brigadier took a swig and set his glass on the table. "Look, Harry, as you have often pointed out, I am not your employer. I can't tell you what to do. But I think it would be wrong to put these people in further danger, or harm's way."

"I agree," I said. "But who are they at risk from?"

The colonel answered. "Well, the six men you plan to eliminate tomorrow, for a start."

"Seven." I turned to the brigadier. "Did you make the call?"

Again the colonel answered. "Yes, I made the call." She nodded as though confirming to herself that she had made the call, then raised her fingers and started counting off the names. "Kit Weiner, Walter de la Potesta, Mahmood Abadi, Senator Bardolino or Judge Williams, any one of them is a potential threat to them."

"Why?"

She leaned forward. "Right now, for no reason, because they are invisible. But if you go and visit them, they become suddenly visible, and vulnerable."

The brigadier cleared his throat.

---

1. See *Breath of Hell*

"Your visit to the judge yesterday, I agree, was necessary. We needed the layout of the room and we needed to know where they would all be sitting. But it also exposed us, however minimally, to your being followed."

"I wasn't followed there and I wasn't followed back."

"That is ninety-nine percent certain. But when we are talking about private citizens, especially people you care about, one percent is too high."

I nodded. "OK, I agree. Where is she?"

The colonel slumped back in her chair. "Six hundred and ninety-something, East Osborn Road. I'll give you the exact address later. Please be careful."

"I don't plan to put her at risk."

"Fine." She sighed. "I'm going up. I'll see you in the morning. I'll put Maggie's address under your door."

She rose, we exchanged good nights and she crossed the lawn into the house. The brigadier lifted his glass and frowned at the amber spirit within.

"I hope your relationship with the colonel is not going to become a problem, Harry."

I drained my glass. "I have no relationship with the colonel, sir."

I went to stand but he said, "That's a lie and you know it." I stared at him with my hands on the arms of my chair. He held my eye. "You don't solve a problem by denying it's there, Harry. Your private life is none of my business, unless it starts to encroach on *our* business." He smiled at me. "I am not unsympathetic. Jane is a very attractive, and very special woman. But this is a relationship —and it *is* a relationship, Harry—that you need to address soon, before it starts to destabilize you—or her."

I was about to stand and walk away, but instead found myself saying, "She has been very hard to talk to since the Yushbaev affair.[2] Pretty unapproachable."

---

2. See *Breath of Hell*

"That's hardly surprising."

He pulled the cork from the whisky and gave me another shot.

"Sure, it must have been very traumatic for her."

"Not just that, Harry." He sat back and sipped his drink. "The lengths you went to for her. What you endured." He paused, frowning at me, like he didn't get that I didn't understand. "We, in the Regiment, do that kind of thing, and we know it's our code. We almost expect it of each other, and of ourselves. We feel gratitude, of course. But it's the code. It's what you do. But for her, Harry, she has no explanation. How is she to explain to herself why you did what you did for her?"

"I had never thought of it like that."

"Well, perhaps you should give it some thought."

We sat in silence for a while, with the liquid moon lapping at the edge of the pool. I smiled, then gave a small laugh. "I used to think that you and she had a thing."

He returned the smile, with a hint of mischief.

"A gentleman doesn't tell." I stared at him with arched eyebrows. He chuckled. "It was very brief, and we both agreed to put Cobra first. But in other circumstances, if I were twenty years younger, it would be pistols at dawn for you and me, me old mucker."

We both laughed. I drained my whisky and wished him a goodnight.

On the way to my room I paused for three very long minutes outside her door before knocking. She opened the door in a bathrobe and we stood looking at each other. Eventually she said, "What do you want, Harry?" and the question seemed to be overloaded with meaning.

"I don't know," I said, honestly expressing myself, the way Bruce Lee had said I should.

She nodded once, sighed, shook her head and took hold of the edge of the door, all in rapid sequence. "Perhaps you should ask Maggie, then."

"If I had wanted to ask her I would have knocked at her door. But I knocked at yours."

"But tomorrow you are going to knock at hers."

"Hell, Jane! We sound like fifteen-year-olds. I have been trying to talk to you since the Yushbaev case, but you have made yourself completely unapproachable."

She looked down at her feet. "I'm sorry if I seem ungrateful."

"Fuck gratitude!"

"Harry!" She frowned. "Your language!"

"To hell with gratitude," I said more quietly. "I didn't imagine what happened in the car after we ate at Keen's, Jane. And, by the way," I smiled ruefully, "if you had come home with me for that nightcap, none of what happened..."

"Stop. No, you didn't imagine what happened in the car, Harry. But I had a lot of time to think while I was Yushbaev's prisoner. And I am just not in the market for a casual on and off relationship with a man who has absolutely no regard for his own safety, or for the..."

She stopped and wiped the back of her wrist across her eyes and then her nose.

"It's late, Harry, and I need to rest." She gave her head a rapid little shake. "Things are just not as simple as you always seem to think they are. Good night."

She closed the door and I made my way to my room.

I WAS UP AT SIX, did an hour of qui gong down by the pool and then spent a half hour doing lengths. At shortly before eight I showered, dressed and had breakfast. The rest of the morning I spent locked in the office with the colonel and the brigadier discussing the plan and all its many ramifications. At twelve we had a light lunch and then went up and started preparing Oz.

It had been my opinion, and the colonel and the brigadier had agreed, that we should rely to an absolute minimum on Oz for the final outcome of the plan, but there was one thing for which I was going to need his cooperation, whether I liked it or not. While he was dressing I told him what it was.

"Oz, there is something that is crucial to the success of this operation."

"I know, I know," he said. "You already told me a hundred times. Make sure they talk about their part in the operation."

"Yeah, aside from that. It is essential that you make sure every single one of you sits around the desk. We are going to be bouncing a laser off the glass in the window by the desk to pick up the conversation."

"Say what?"

"It's called a laser microphone. Now this whole thing goes to hell, and you along with it, if we cannot record the conversation. So, I have seen where he has his desk, and I need you all sitting around that desk, by the window. Understood?"

"You got it, general. Anything else?"

"If you can make those two things happen, I'll be happy."

"That's all I want, Harry, to make you happy."

He stood and pulled his shirt over the mass of bandages and plaster that encased his abdomen and his chest.

"It had better be, Oscar, because this deal only holds if we get good audio and a good recording that can convict these bastards."

"Yeah." He gave several exaggerated nods, and stared at me fixedly. "I think I got that, chief. I'm intuitive that way. Know what I'm saying?"

We made our way down the stairs and out to the garage, where Oz climbed into the passenger seat of the dark Range Rover, and I got in behind the wheel. The automatic door rose on a glaring Arizona morning and we pulled out into the heat of the day.

We wound down out of the Fountain Hills and took East Shea Boulevard as far as North Scottsdale, where we turned south. At Doubletree Ranch Road we turned west and then turned south again on North 56th.

The judge's mansion rose like an oxblood behemoth,

dwarfing the houses either side of it. Two guys in suits stood at the gate with wires in their ears and lumps under their jackets. They confirmed who we were, spoke on their walky-talkies and the big gate rolled back. I drove in. Oz spoke for the first time since we'd left the brigadier's place.

"You have to come up?"

"Yes."

"Can't you just let me do this my way?"

"No. Now shut up and get out."

The two guards had come in with us and the gate had closed behind them. One of them had a platinum crew cut. The other had a dark crew cut. The one with the platinum crew cut said, "Follow me."

We followed him and retraced the route I had made before. At the big, oak door he tapped and stepped in.

"Oscar Larsen and Harry Field," he said, then stepped back and held the door for us.

We went in and there they were, all five of them, sitting around the large desk. The platinum crew cut withdrew and the judge looked at me with something like hatred.

"Do you intend to be part of this meeting?"

"No."

I looked around the table, trying to identify who was who. Senator Geordi Bardolino was easy. He had the permed hair with the graying temples, the navy blazer and the gray chinos, and "senator" written all over his face. Walter de la Potesta I knew from seeing him on the TV. He was gaunt, hollow-eyed and had a look of depravity about him. That left Mahmood Abadi, who was clearly the heavy-set Arab who was watching me through slightly yellow eyes, and Kit Weiner, the scrawny guy with the mop of curly hair.

I said, "I am just here to see that he's OK, and to lay some ground rules." I pointed at the desk. "You sit at this table. You do not move from this table. You hold your discussion in a businesslike and timely manner, you reach your agreement and when your business is done, he leaves without obstruction or incident. If there is any kind of problem, be assured that hell will rain down on you gentlemen," I paused for effect, "...and your families."

The judge snapped, "Where is the ledger?"

Oz laughed and sat himself down in the one empty chair. It was clear he was going to enjoy himself.

He looked up at me with something very like contempt and said, "I got this, Harry. I'll see you in the car in fifteen minutes." He grinned at the judge. "Maybe twenty if the judge offers us one of his fine single malts."

I stepped out of the room and closed the door behind me. I trotted down the grotesque, caracole stairs to the vast, white marble entrance hall and out into the sun. I slipped on my shades and climbed into the Range Rover. The gates slid open and I slipped through.

I pulled out onto Mockingbird Lane with my windows down. As the gates closed behind me, my cell rang. I answered it and the brigadier said, "I have just had confirmation that Abdul ben Elahi was stabbed and strangled in the showers this morning. They suspect the Sons of Odin, a white-supremacist grudge thing."

"That's a great loss to online education."

"Yes."

He hung up and I cruised one-handed as I scrolled through my speed-dials. There I found and pressed the number nine, and slowed, leaning and listening at the window. The report was muffled, but loud enough. I stopped as I turned into North 59th Street. The oxblood atrocity was concealed from view by an abundance of trees, but a column of black smoke was curling up into the bright blue, blue sky.

I cruised down North 58th aiming ultimately to make Invergordon Road. I called the brigadier. "I heard it. Did you get visual?"

"Yes, we launched the spy-drone from North Caballo Drive. We had visual at the time of the blast. It blew out the window and tore off part of the roof."

"They were all at the desk?"

"Yes. Nobody survived."

"OK, I'll see you in a couple of hours, maybe a little more."

One and a half pounds of C4—what I had left over from New Mexico—laced with ball bearings and detonated in an enclosed place, had had a devastating effect. Especially for Oz, who had, unwittingly, been wearing the lethal compound folded into the plaster around his waist and his chest. There had been no cracked ribs, not before he put on the plaster, anyhow. Now, I figured, he had a few.

I eventually found my way to North Scottsdale Road and cruised gently south among the broad, low buildings, the tall palms and the ever-present red sand. At Walgreens I turned right onto Osborn and began to smile. A couple of minutes later I pulled up outside a pretty, suburban house with a white porch and a well-tended lawn.

I climbed out of the Range Rover and walked slowly to the door. It opened before I could ring the bell. Maggie was smiling up at me, reeking of harvests and home-baked apple pie. Inside I could just hear the sound of the Roadrunner and the Wily Coyote on the TV.

She smiled and bit her lip, then cocked a hip. "I thought you was never going to show."

"Now that I'm here, what are you going to do about it?"

"Guess I'll have to take you inside and give you some of my mom's extra special apple pie."

I raised an eyebrow and said, quietly, "Yeehaa..."

**Don't miss THE SHADOW OF UKUPACHA. The riveting sequel
in the Harry Bauer Thriller series.**

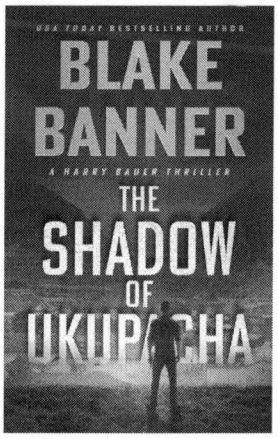

Scan the QR code below to purchase THE SHADOW OF
UKUPACHA.

Or go to: righthouse.com/the-shadow-of-ukupacha

NOTE: flip to the very end to read an exclusive sneak peak...

DON'T MISS ANYTHING!

If you want to stay up to date on all new releases in this series, with this author, or with any of our new deals, you can do so by joining our newsletters below.

In addition, you will immediately gain access to our entire *Right House VIP Library,* which includes many riveting Mystery and Thriller novels for your enjoyment!

righthouse.com/email

(Easy to unsubscribe. No spam. Ever.)

ALSO BY BLAKE BANNER

Up to date books can be found at:
www.righthouse.com/blake-banner

ROGUE THRILLERS
Gates of Hell (Book 1)
Hell's Fury (Book 2)

ALEX MASON THRILLERS
Odin (Book 1)
Ice Cold Spy (Book 2)
Mason's Law (Book 3)
Assets and Liabilities (Book 4)
Russian Roulette (Book 5)
Executive Order (Book 6)
Dead Man Talking (Book 7)
All The King's Men (Book 8)
Flashpoint (Book 9)
Brotherhood of the Goat (Book 10)
Dead Hot (Book 11)
Blood on Megiddo (Book 12)
Son of Hell (Book 13)

HARRY BAUER THRILLER SERIES
Dead of Night (Book 1)
Dying Breath (Book 2)
The Einstaat Brief (Book 3)
Quantum Kill (Book 4)
Immortal Hate (Book 5)
The Silent Blade (Book 6)
LA: Wild Justice (Book 7)

Breath of Hell (Book 8)
Invisible Evil (Book 9)
The Shadow of Ukupacha (Book 10)
Sweet Razor Cut (Book 11)
Blood of the Innocent (Book 12)
Blood on Balthazar (Book 13)
Simple Kill (Book 14)
Riding The Devil (Book 15)
The Unavenged (Book 16)
The Devil's Vengeance (Book 17)
Bloody Retribution (Book 18)
Rogue Kill (Book 19)
Blood for Blood (Book 20)

DEAD COLD MYSTERY SERIES
An Ace and a Pair (Book 1)
Two Bare Arms (Book 2)
Garden of the Damned (Book 3)
Let Us Prey (Book 4)
The Sins of the Father (Book 5)
Strange and Sinister Path (Book 6)
The Heart to Kill (Book 7)
Unnatural Murder (Book 8)
Fire from Heaven (Book 9)
To Kill Upon A Kiss (Book 10)
Murder Most Scottish (Book 11)
The Butcher of Whitechapel (Book 12)
Little Dead Riding Hood (Book 13)
Trick or Treat (Book 14)
Blood Into Wine (Book 15)
Jack In The Box (Book 16)
The Fall Moon (Book 17)
Blood In Babylon (Book 18)
Death In Dexter (Book 19)
Mustang Sally (Book 20)

A Christmas Killing (Book 21)
Mommy's Little Killer (Book 22)
Bleed Out (Book 23)
Dead and Buried (Book 24)
In Hot Blood (Book 25)
Fallen Angels (Book 26)
Knife Edge (Book 27)
Along Came A Spider (Book 28)
Cold Blood (Book 29)
Curtain Call (Book 30)

THE OMEGA SERIES
Dawn of the Hunter (Book 1)
Double Edged Blade (Book 2)
The Storm (Book 3)
The Hand of War (Book 4)
A Harvest of Blood (Book 5)
To Rule in Hell (Book 6)
Kill: One (Book 7)
Powder Burn (Book 8)
Kill: Two (Book 9)
Unleashed (Book 10)
The Omicron Kill (Book 11)
9mm Justice (Book 12)
Kill: Four (Book 13)
Death In Freedom (Book 14)
Endgame (Book 15)

ABOUT US

Right House is an independent publisher created by authors for readers. We specialize in Action, Thriller, Mystery, and Crime novels.

If you enjoyed this novel, then there is a good chance you will like what else we have to offer! Please stay up to date by using any of the links below.

Join our mailing lists to stay up to date -->
righthouse.com/email
Visit our website --> righthouse.com
Contact us --> contact@righthouse.com

 facebook.com/righthousebooks
 x.com/righthousebooks
 instagram.com/righthousebooks

EXCLUSIVE SNEAK PEAK OF...

THE SHADOW OF UKUPACHA

CHAPTER 1

I WAS IN DC BECAUSE SENATOR RANDY ORTEGA HAD told the brigadier he wanted to discuss a "sensitive issue." When a senator tells the head of COBRA that he wants to discuss a "sensitive issue," it means there's somebody he wants eliminated. That's what COBRA does, it eliminates people who commit crimes against humanity, but are beyond the reach of the law. What was unusual, though, was that he had asked me to come along too. Usually the client uses the brigadier and the colonel to mediate. That way they don't get their hands dirty by associating with the executioner.

That's me, the executioner.

Senator Ortega's office was in the Old House Office Building, a name that belied the understated elegance and grandeur of the edifice on Independence Avenue, in the United States Capitol Complex. I arrived by cab and met the brigadier among marble echoes in the rotunda. He greeted me with a nod and we walked together without speaking, down the left-hand passage and around the dogleg, to the senator's office. There we entered the antechamber, guarded by his secretary. She had a mouth like a razorblade and blue eyes that doubled as stabbing instruments.

She was a living paradox in that she displaced her body from one location to another, while taking care not to move any part of it.

"The senator is expecting you, brigadier," she said, as though it were a grievous accusation, "go right on in." She pressed a button and the door buzzed and clunked softly. The brigadier pushed it open and we went inside. The door clunked behind us.

The office was large and had broad windows overlooking First Street. The floor was carpeted in royal blue, the furniture was all dark mahogany and oak, the walls were partially paneled in paler oak, and burgundy leather armchairs and a sofa occupied the space before an open fireplace. The senator was behind the desk, and behind him was the flag of the Unites States, and a photograph of the president, whom he did not support.

He stood as we entered and gave a comfortable laugh as he reached out for the brigadier's hand.

"Buddy! Good to see you. How've you been?" He grabbed the brigadier's hand with both of his own and pumped it, then looked at me and grinned.

"Harry! You mind if I call you Harry?"

We shook and I smiled. "It's preferable to what a lot of other people call me."

He gave a little jump when he laughed. He laughed loud, staring at the brigadier and then back at me.

"Those who are still alive, huh? Huh?" He laughed again, and feinted a punch at my chest. "You know what we call you 'round here? Those of us who know? We call you the 'H-bomb.' The H-bomb! Huh?"

The brigadier made for a chair with an unamused rictus on his face.

"I'd rather you didn't talk about him at all, Randy. Black coffee, please."

Randy shrugged and spread his hands. "I know, I know. It's just the few of us in the know. The H-bomb, it's good." He returned behind his desk and pressed a button. "Hey, Melinda, coffee for three, black. Sit."

This last was directed at me. The brigadier had already sat. I lowered myself into a comfortable leather armchair and he dropped into a black leather swivel chair that was probably big enough for his whole family to share.

I was getting bored with the polite preambles so I interrupted whatever it was he was about to say.

"Senator, it is extremely unusual for me, or any man in my position, to be invited to a meeting. Why am I here?"

He looked at me from under his eyebrows. "Talks like he shoots, huh? Straight to the point."

"Time is the one thing we can't restock."

He nodded like he agreed. "I don't know if you know much about me," he gestured at the brigadier with both hands, "or if Buddy has told you about my special interests...?"

"I know you were involved with the UFO disclosure movement. I'm afraid it's an issue that doesn't interest me much, so that's about all I do know." He hesitated a moment and I frowned and added, "If that is relevant here, I think maybe you have the wrong man."

He glanced at the brigadier who remained silent, then looked back at me.

"Don't worry, I'm not going to send you off to assassinate Paul." I arched an eyebrow which said I had no idea what he was talking about. He said, "Paul? The movie? No? Forget it. Listen, I am in Harry Reid's gang, but I'm definitely not into tinfoil hats and all that shit. I am briefed by the UAPTF and other very serious agencies, and I also have a special interest in what we might call the History of the American People. The way I see it, the fockin' Europeans..."

He paused with his mouth sagging open and grinned at the brigadier. "Sorry, Buddy, but you're not European anymore, right?"

"Right."

"Good, so the fockin' Europeans want a fockin' monopoly over history, because that makes them more fockin' civilized. You know what I'm sayin'? Man first appears in Africa, then moves into Europe and becomes super-advanced, democratic, technological, yadda yadda, and then, and only then, moves to the so-called 'New World.' Bullshit! Bull-shit! I got news for you—not for you, but for them. We were building pyramids and cities in America, with super-advanced technologies, when in Europe they were still learning to make huts out of wattle and daub. You know what I'm saying?"

"Sure, but I still don't get what this has to do with me. You want me to take out all the European historians?"

"I'm getting there. You have somewhere you need to be?" I made the face of patience and shook my head once. "So chill. And by the way," he grinned, "that wouldn't be a bad idea at all."

The door opened and Melinda came in, managing to walk and carry a tray while still not moving. She set the tray down on the desk and left.

"Enjoy the coffee and relax. This is about blood." He picked up his cup and sipped. "You guys, your ancestors come from Europe," he gestured at the brigadier, "not him. He comes from Britain, the smallest continent on Earth, but for us Latinos, with Indian blood, having our past robbed from us hurts. A lot of my constituents are Mexican, I got others from Colombia, Peru, and some Native North Americans too. And we feel that history is being deliberately manipulated to hide what was going on in America in ancient prehistory."

I sipped my coffee. He went on.

"So, I was active, and instrumental, in persuading the American Indian Studies Department of the University of Arizona to fund a dig in Peru, just outside San Julian, in the Convención province, in the region of Cusco. The dig is being supervised by a constituent of mine, who also happens to be a close friend, Dr. Elizabeth Caldwell. And I am here to tell you, pal, what they are digging up there, in the mountains above the Urubamba River, will blow your mind. I mean really blow your mind."

He watched for a response and got none, so he pressed on.

"OK, so at the same time, in the same town of San Julian, while Liz is up Mount Apusupay making the discovery that will turn our whole understanding of human history on its head, deep in the San Julian Valley, at the bottom of the San Julian Gorge, in dense rainforest, Dr. Amanda Epstein is conducting revolutionary, and highly secret, biochemical research on behalf of the Pasqüal Pharmaceutical Company of Munich. And before you ask, I have no idea what they are doing there."

I placed my empty cup on his desk and said, "OK, Senator, you have set the scene. Now, please, how do I fit into all this?"

He scowled at me a moment. "I thought you ninja guys were supposed to have infinite patience."

"I am not a ninja. I was with the British SAS and we tended to get things done fast and with a minimum of fuss and distraction."

"OK, Harry, just relax, everything I am telling you is relevant."

He pulled open a drawer in his desk and took out a transparent, plastic wallet. Inside it was a plain white envelope with a handwritten address on it in red ink. Beside that was a single sheet of paper. At a glance I could see it was also handwritten, all in caps and, oddly, in various different-colored inks.

The senator reached in the drawer again and removed three pairs of latex gloves from a pack. He tossed one pair to the brigadier and another to me. Then he pulled on his own pair and removed the contents from the transparent sheath. He slid the envelope across the desk to me.

"What do you make of that? The stamp and postmark are from Cusco, Peru. Sent two weeks ago. The address is written in capitals, in red ink, and despite the capitalization, personally, I think you can make out a childish, unformed hand."

"The use of red ink is also odd," I said.

"Yeah, I want to come back to that. See the letter?" He slipped it in front of me. "I'm going to give you a copy to take away with you. He uses four different colors of ink: blue, black, red and green. Here he switches in the middle of the paragraph. I don't know, maybe he was running out of ink. There seems to be no reason for the switches. He's not emphasizing anything. It seems to be random, but I think he was trying to tell me something. Something specific."

I picked it up and started to read it. I spoke as I read. "Like what? Color coding the information? Trying to draw your attention to certain paragraphs? Seems a complicated and unreliable way of doing it."

"Read it, then we'll talk about the ink."

I read:

Dear Senator Ortega,

I am writing to you because I know how important American Indian history is for you. And I know that you have invested a lot of time and effort in making this excavation happen. But you should know that this is not the Golden Opportunity you thought. Some very bad things are happening here. People are dying. People are being taken into slavery. Women and children. People are having their souls sucked out and eaten by daemons.

There is awful evil at work here, Senator, and somebody has to look into it and do something about it. Danny tried talking to the alcalde and to the police in Cusco, but they said he was crazy. I have been warned to be quiet too, or I will die like Danny, or worse.

Please, Senator Ortega, do something. Danny tried and Danny died. Supay is coming in the tunnels and the deep caves, Senator, coming up from Ukupacha, and they will eat our souls. They will poison us first, with nuna miyu, and then they will eat our souls. They will eat all our souls, until no man and no woman on Earth is left with his soul.

Danny tried to warn, but Danny died. Soon we will all be living in death.

Look for me, I will show you.

Carl Allen

. . .

I LAID the letter down and looked into the senator's eyes. "OK, so you are taking this guy seriously and I wonder why. He is probably psychotic, or he is perpetrating a hoax. So what is making you give credence to what he is saying?"

He pointed at me. "That, see? That is the right question. And the answer is, there are two reasons. One, this guy is not crazy."

"You know him?"

"No, but he knows me. This is strictly between us. When I was much younger, I was a conspiracy nut, and I got involved in an investigation into an alleged experiment conducted by the US Navy involving Einstein's unified field theory, and a lot of weird shit that went down toward the end of the war. Anyhow, the whistle blower in that case, who tried to blow the lid off the experiments, was called Carl Allen. Now, Carl Allen wrote several letters to one Morris Jessup, in exactly this way: by hand and in various different-colored inks. The letters read like he was a schizophrenic, but much of what he said turned out..." He paused. "Well, never mind. The point is nobody knows anymore that I was involved in that investigation. But this Carl Allen clearly does. And in writing the letter in this way, he is telling me that this is an issue of similar importance."

"You investigated that experiment alone?"

"No, there were a couple of other people involved. They have all moved on and occupy positions in society."

I arched an eyebrow at him. "Any of them have kids who are studying archeology?"

"We all swore each other to secrecy."

I shook my head. "An oath of secrecy is as solid as the last glass of wine you drank. Kids meet in college, 'You'll never guess, I heard my dad telling a friend last night Senator Ortega used to be a UFO nut.' You may find all this compelling, Senator, but I'm afraid I don't."

"I didn't think you would, Harry. But the second reason will carry more weight with you. I made," he hesitated, "uh, discreet inquiries, through Liz, and she did have a boy working for her on the dig, a graduate student from Arizona, whose name was Danny Cooper. He became depressed about six months ago, climbed to the top of the Apusupay Mountain and threw himself off, into the Urubamba River."

"Danny Cooper? He wouldn't be any relation to Edwin Cooper, the Aerospace billionaire?"

He grunted and sighed. He delivered his answer to the brigadier. "He is like you described him." To me he said, "OK, so you do your homework. Good. Yeah, Ed was a friend of mine back in the day..."

"And like you he still has an interest in all things outer space. Wasn't he awarded a contract by the Air Force to carry out research into the ion drive recently?"

"Yes."

"So is he any relation to Danny Cooper."

"Ed is Danny's father. So I have a personal interest in this. Danny was almost a nephew to me."

I turned to look at the brigadier. He avoided my eye and gazed out of the window. I sighed and turned back to Ortega.

"Senator, what is it exactly you want me to do? Frankly, I think what you have here is a bunch of kids who have been too long in the remote areas of Peru. They have probably been visiting local paq yachaq, experimenting with mind-altering substances and gone out of their minds. Edwin Cooper told his son you had both investigated the Philadelphia Experiment together. When Danny died, one of his pals, suffering paranoia from too much ayahuasca, wrote to you as Carl Allen. It sucks, but that is not the kind of stuff we deal with, Senator. We deal with people who commit crimes against humanity. That's our remit."

He nodded, then he looked at his desktop and nodded some more.

"I know that, Harry. I can't tell you how or why, but I can tell you for certain that Carl Allen, in this letter, is warning me that there is a crime being committed against humanity even as we speak, down in the San Julian Valley. More than that, if we do not act soon, an even greater crime is going to be committed."

I sighed again, a little louder. "That the Supay, the spirits of the underworld, are going to rise up from Ukupacha, the underworld, and eat everybody's soul? You don't need me, Senator. You need Fox Mulder from the FBI."

"Don't get smart with me, Harry. You have to take it as read that I know what I am talking about. And the brigadier here will vouch for that."

I turned to look at the brigadier. He was watching me impassively. After a moment he nodded.

"I have known the senator for many years, Harry. He has been a client on many occasions, and I have never known him to be wrong. He has his sources, and I know them to be very reliable."

I scowled. "So what's the job? Track down the god of the underworld and kill him?"

The senator stared at me a moment. He looked mad. Then suddenly he laughed. He turned and laughed at the brigadier, pointing at me.

"Insolent focking son of a bitch. Ha! Ha! Ha!"

He stopped laughing as suddenly as he had started and said, "Yeah, pretty much that is what I want. Find Carl Allen, find out who he is and what he is talking about. Find out what he means by 'eating souls,' find out who's doing it and kill them."

"Do I get a choice in this?"

He cleared his throat and started fitting the letter and the envelope back in the plastic sleeve. I looked at the brigadier. He shook his head.

"OK, so when do I leave?"

The senator reached in another drawer and pulled out a large white envelope, which he dropped in front of me.

"Courtesy of the Central Intelligence Agency. Everything you need is in there. Go do what you do best, Harry. Buddy here will keep me posted."

I took the envelope and inspected the contents: a passport, a driver's permit and a credit card in the name of Henry Baumb—cute—a first-class ticket to Cusco and a slim manila file.

I stood. The brigadier and the senator exchanged handshakes, good wishes and a few shoulder-slaps, and we left the office in silence.

We walked down the echoing, marble corridor as far as the great, vaulted rotunda and stepped out into the bright sunshine, opposite the Capitol. There I stopped and the brigadier turned to face me. I spoke before he did.

"I thought we had an understanding. I choose my jobs. You are not my boss, sir. I don't work for you and this is not the army. And this..." I held up the manila envelope. "This job is bullshit!"

"Harry—"

He said it quietly, but he had that kind of authority that made you shut up and listen even if he only whispered. So I shut up and listened.

"In the first place Senator Ortega has the kind of pull that could put our budget in jeopardy. So you'll understand that I don't want to upset him, unless I have to."

"If you had to, would you?"

He didn't hesitate. "Yes. I will not compromise our principles or the way we operate."

"Isn't that exactly what you have just done?"

"No. And if you'll listen for a moment I'll explain why."

"Go ahead."

He looked away at the traffic cruising down the broad expanse of Independence Avenue. For a long moment he didn't speak. When he did he locked eyes with me.

"In the second place, Harry, I have a strong feeling that there is a lot more to this case than meets the eye. If you don't want to do it you don't have to. I'll face the music. But I want my best man on this. I don't want a professional killer with ice in his veins. I want a blade, a trooper from the Regiment, who can assess the situation and act accordingly."

There was no mistaking the seriousness in his voice. I narrowed my eyes.

"You're serious. What do you think is going on down there? You don't believe all this Aztec god's revenge crap, do you?"

"No." He blinked a couple of times. "But something is going on, and I want to know what. I would consider it a personal favor if you go and check it out. I also think you'll find there are deeper depths and levels than you suspect."

"Seriously?"

"Ortega discussed this case with...people; people who know about Cobra. They all agreed they wanted you to take the case. There is a lot more to this than meets the eye, Harry. Look into it, find out what is going on, and if you judge an execution is in order, you have the authority to carry it out."

"Judge, jury and executioner?"

He held my eye. "Is it the first time in your career you've had to do that?"

I thought about it. "No." And then, "OK, I'll do it."

CHAPTER 2

COLONEL JANE HARRIS, COBRA'S HEAD OF Operations, lived in a large, Victorian house on Potomac Avenue, a stone's throw from the Army's Dalecarlia Water Treatment Plant and the Renaissance Sibley Hospital. It was an elegant, yellow-brick, two-story affair with an elaborate wrought-iron veranda on both floors, which gave it a kind of colonial feel. It had a well-kept lawn out front bordered by thuja trees and rosebushes, and abundant trees poking over the black slate, gabled roof.

I sat in my TVR, staring at the house and wondering what the hell I was doing there. It was tacitly understood that though she was Head of Operations, the brigadier briefed me, and she and I kept our distance. It was a wise arrangement, and yet.

I climbed out of the beast, slammed the door and followed the stone path to the yellow brick house. There I leaned on the bell for a few seconds, and waited, detecting noises inside.

She opened the door and frowned at me. She was in Levi's, Converse trainers and a blue and white checked shirt. She looked like a '50s ad for milk. I smiled at her frown.

"Is this a bad time?"

She blinked hard and frowned harder. "Uh, no... Harry, what are you doing here?"

I shrugged. "I'm flying out tomorrow. Apparently there is a good chance I will have my soul sucked out and eaten by the Supay. I'm still not clear if that's a 'him' or a 'them,' but either way, he or they are coming up from Ukupacha, and I may get my soul eaten. I thought maybe I'd better come and say goodbye."

She stood staring up at me a moment, then added a sigh to make me feel a little bit more uncomfortable. I said, "If this is a bad time, you have company or anything..."

"It's not a bad time, Harry, and I haven't got company. Even if I had, it wouldn't matter. But..." She raised her open hands, then let them drop. "You'd better come in."

She stood back and I stepped inside. "Sure know how to make a guy feel welcome." I added a smile to show there was no hard feeling. She didn't respond and I followed her into her living room, where she sat on an elegant sage sofa which was looking good for its age. I figured a century at least.

She got straight to the point. "Harry, you know what the situation is."

"Are you going to ask me to sit down, or do I have to take this standing up?"

"Don't be absurd."

She gestured with a limp hand and a sage chair that matched the sage sofa, and shifted her butt so she was looking at me when I sat.

"Harry, you know what this job entails. You know we can't allow personal feelings to intrude."

I did something that ended up being a hybrid of a snort and a smile.

"I don't want to marry you, Jane. I was in DC, I expected you to be at the briefing. I thought I'd look in and see how you are. You're the Head of Operations, but I have barely seen you since the Yushbaev affair.[1]"

---

1. See *Breath of Hell*

She looked away. "You keep harping back to that, as though I don't feel guilty enough."

"There is no reason for you to feel guilty. You did what any mother would have done. Jane, this doesn't have to be complicated. We just..."

"It is complicated, Harry! Whether it has to be or not. We operate in a very tenuous gray area in the law, we cannot be like other people. We cannot behave like other people, and we certainly can't..."

She stopped herself.

"Can't what?"

She let her gaze drop to the floor and spoke softly. "We can't behave like ordinary people. Let's just leave it at that."

I said, "We can't even be friends?" and kicked myself for sounding like some lame, Californian high school soap.

She tried to look at me, but her eyes wound up staring out the window.

"The brigadier and I have spoken."

"That sounds ominous."

"We've discussed it, and we both agree it is probably best if you and I keep our contact to a minimum."

I felt the hot twist of anger in my gut. "Don't you think I would have been a better person to discuss that with?"

Now she looked at me, and her eyes were bright and angry and sad all at the same time.

"No! That's precisely it, Harry! You don't get it. This is not about you or me, it's about Cobra! And the work we do. You, me, our feelings, they are irrelevant! That is the whole point. So no, I should definitely not discuss it with you. I should discuss it with the brigadier because with this behavior, what you are doing right now, we are putting Cobra at risk. Your being here now puts Cobra at risk."

"So I should leave?"

Again her eyes went to the carpet.

"Yes, you should."

"Fine." I stood. "I am sorry I came and caused you embarrassment." Her eyes closed in a wince of pain. Anger and hurt drove me on. "I assure you it won't happen again."

I left her house with the hot burn of humiliation in my belly and in my cheeks. I drove back to my hotel on Maryland Avenue, ordered a sirloin steak and a bottle of mineral water, and studied the file the senator had given me, while I ate lunch on my balcony, overlooking the circus.

The file wasn't much: pictures of Liz Calder, pretty, blonde, thirty-something, a face that had grown accustomed to looking worried and defensive; pictures of Danny Cooper, the beach boy American dream, surfer, quarterback with a brain, honorable, good listener, all the girls are in love with him. I wondered if that included Liz Calder, and whether it was relevant.

More pictures, a couple of Alfredo Quispe, the mayor of San Julian, friend to foreigners, especially those with dollars, local landowner and patron of archeologists.

There wasn't a lot besides that. I had been booked in at Angie's Hostal in the town square, which was rather unimaginatively called Plaza de San Julian. The booking form told me I not only got my own bathroom and WiFi, I also got hot water twenty-four hours a day.

My weapons, a Sig Sauer P226 TacOps and a Fairbairn and Sykes commando fighting knife, had been sent on ahead to the hostel with special diplomatic customs clearance. According to the file Liz Calder and some of her team were also staying at Angie's.

I finished my meal, packed my case and spent a couple of hours in the hotel gym, working with weights to enhance power and speed. When I had finished my routine and I was headed for the showers a guy in his late twenties, with an unfashionable moustache and a chest like a beer vat, smiled at me and rose from the bench where he was doing sit-ups. I'd noticed he'd done about five hundred. He was sweating, but he wasn't out of breath.

"Excuse me—"

I looked at him and waited. He said, "Are you Harry Bauer?"

"Yeah, why?"

"I apologize for intruding, my name is Frank Cooper. Folks call me Frankie. Look, um..."

Every alarm bell in my body was ringing. "You have my attention, Mr. Cooper. What's on your mind?"

"Yeah, I'm sorry." He ran his fingers through his hair. "It's a kind of delicate subject. Could we talk somewhere private?"

I mopped my face with my towel and sighed. "Probably not. How long is this going to take?"

He held up his hands like I was going to shoot him. "Five, ten minutes most. It's about my brother."

"Danny."

His eyes widened. "Yes, you know?"

"Meet me in the cocktail lounge at seven. You've got ten minutes."

"Thank you, Mr. Bauer. I am truly grateful."

I skipped the shower, went up to my room, showered there and changed for dinner. At six-fifty I was down in the cocktail lounge leaning up against the bar. The place was quiet, so Johnny, the New York barman, sidled over and jerked his chin at me.

"You're from New York, right?"

"Born and bred."

"So you know the New York alphabet."

He was wiping down the bar, watching me. I shook my head. "Can't say I do."

"C'mon," he said in mock exasperation, "fuckin' A, fuckin' B, fuckin' C." I laughed. "That's the New York alphabet, man. What'll it be?"

"The Macallan, straight up." As he set up the glass I asked him, "You want to make an easy C-note?"

"Who do I have to kill?"

"Nothing that complicated. A nervous kid with a moustache is going to join me in about five minutes. When he's done with his drink, don't wash his glass, just put it in a plastic bag for me."

His eyebrows crawled up his balding head. "That's it?"

I grinned without humor. "I want to know if he's the father of my daughter's baby."

"He says he's not?"

"Son of a bitch."

"Consider it done. I always charge in advance. Company policy."

I slipped him a hundred dollars which he pocketed and poured me a generous measure of Scotch. A couple of minutes later Frank Cooper came into the bar, like a hesitant chicken, looking left and right before every step. I hailed him, he looked relieved and joined me as I sat at a table in the corner.

"Thanks again for seeing me, Mr. Bauer. I realize you must be a busy man."

"What makes you say that?"

He looked startled, and as he fumbled for an answer I watched his pupils, his complexion and the skin on his neck. I didn't see anything unusual. He finished up on, "I just assume, a man of your um, uh, standing, would be... I mean, I didn't mean anything by it, I just..."

"Say what you mean, mean what you say, Mr. Cooper. Now, what about your brother?"

"Oh, uh, Danny?"

I narrowed my eyes and looked for changes in his breathing, trembling of the hands. There was nothing at all.

"That's what you said, Mr. Cooper. You said Danny was your brother. Are you nervous for some reason?"

"No, well, yeah, a bit."

The waitress came over and smiled a question at Cooper. He said, "Oh, um...Coke," he gave a nervous laugh, "No zeros, just normal..."

"Original."

"That's the one."

She went away and he looked at me across the table. Before he could say, "Oh, um…" again I said, "What's making you nervous, Mr. Cooper?"

He looked at his hands cupped in his lap. "I don't know if you know it, Mr. Bauer, but you're a pretty intimidating guy."

"I know it," I said without inflection. "So how about we start with you telling me how you know who I am?"

He thought about it for a moment and now I saw his neck color slightly.

"My dad was in Delta Force."

"So what?"

The waitress brought over his Coke and set it in front of him with another cute smile.

"He did a few training exercises with the SAS. He said he met you on one of the exercises."

I allowed my mind to flow backward, searching for a Cooper. There was a Frank Cooper, years back, almost at the beginning. I barely remembered him.

"What was his name?"

"Frank, like me."

"How the hell does your father know I'm in DC?"

"He saw you this morning, at Cannon House. He's head of security there."

I leaned forward. "First, how the hell did he see me and I didn't see him?"

"He saw you on camera and after a moment he recognized you."

"Second, why are you talking to me instead of him?"

"He was going to, but he thought it would attract too much attention, so he checked the visitors' log and saw where you were staying." I sat back in my seat. It was credible. He went on, "Dad said that if anybody could find out what happened to Danny, you could."

I shook my head. It was too much of a coincidence. "He must know a hundred guys as good as me."

"No." He shook his head with feeling. "He said the guys you

were with, Captain Walker, Sergeant Hays, Sergeant Gordon and you, were the best he'd ever seen."

I sipped my whisky and as I set the glass down I asked him, "So what's your brother done?"

"He's dead."

"There's not much I can do for him, then, is there?"

"But Dad, and me, we want to know what happened. He was down in Peru, on an archeological dig, he was enjoying himself." He gave a small laugh. "It was like a dream come true for him. He was crazy about archeology, especially the Incas and the Maya and all that. But one day he grabs one of the Jeeps, drives to the top of the mountain where the dig was, and just throws himself off. Why would he do that?"

I scowled at him. "I don't know. Why would I? What is it exactly you and your dad expect me to do?"

"Look," he swallowed hard, "my dad knows that you're going to Peru, to investigate the dig." He held up both hands like I might be about to hit him. "He doesn't know why! He doesn't know any details. But he knows you're going, and he's willing to pay, whatever price you name, if you'll find out what happened to Danny."

I narrowed my eyes and shook my head, thinking fast. "You must be out of your mind, both of you. I don't know what you're talking about."

I was about to stand, but he stopped me. "I have information that will be useful to you."

"What information?"

"Letters, letters Danny sent us just before he died. He said there was something weird going on. He didn't know what it was. It's best if you read them."

"Get the hell out of here. I'm going to have dinner. Come to my room at ten and bring the letters. I'll give you an answer then."

He nodded eagerly. "Thank you, Mr. Bauer. I am incredibly grateful. Thank you so much."

"Shut up. You're making a scene. Go."

I took my time over dinner, thinking things through from every angle. At nine-fifty I ordered a Macallan and told the waiter I'd be right back, I had forgotten something in my room. I was unlocking the door when Cooper appeared climbing the stairs. He approached me in silence. I pushed the door open and indicated he should go inside. I left the door open and followed him as far as the desk, where he reached into his inside pocket.

I put my left hand firmly on his right wrist, pressing it hard against his chest, and smashed a right hook hard into his floating ribs. As he doubled up, wheezing, I reached inside his jacket, for whatever it was he was reaching for.

As I had expected, there were no letters. There was a long, razor-sharp stiletto in a slim holster under his arm. I grabbed him by the scruff of his neck and the seat of his pants, rushed him to the balcony and heaved him over. He didn't scream, he was winded, but he did make a sickening thud.

"Do your homework, schmuck," I told him, too late for it to be of any use. "Danny's father was Edwin, not Frank."

I went down to the dining room and finished my Scotch, wondering what it meant.

Scan the QR code below to purchase THE SHADOW OF UKUPACHA.
Or go to: righthouse.com/the-shadow-of-ukupacha

Made in United States
Orlando, FL
02 January 2026

76166249R10132